'I don't see an

'Just admit that th
and put me on the f

'The problem, my bad-tempered little sea-witch, is the mutual sexual attraction we seem to have for each other. The more I think of that, the more I find myself weighing it in your favour.'

Dear Reader

The first few months of a new year are a time for looking forward and wondering what the future holds for us. There are no such worries when you pick up a Mills & Boon story, though—you're guaranteed to find an exciting, heart-warming romance! This month, as usual, we've got some real treats in store for you. So, whatever 1995 brings you, you can be sure of one thing: if you're reading Mills & Boon, it's going to be a year of romance!

The Editor

Alex Ryder was born and raised in Edinburgh and is married with three sons. She took an interest in writing when, to her utter amazement, she won a national schools competition for a short essay about wild birds. She prefers writing romantic fiction because at heart she's just a big softie. She works now in close collaboration with a scruffy old one-eyed cat who sits on the desk and yawns when she doesn't get it right, but winks when she does.

Recent titles by the same author:

DARK AVENGER

SHORES
OF LOVE

BY
ALEX RYDER

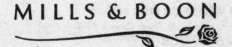

MILLS & BOON LIMITED
ETON HOUSE, 18-24 PARADISE ROAD
RICHMOND, SURREY TW9 1SR

MILLS & BOON and the Rose Device are trademarks of the publisher.

First published in Great Britain 1995 by Mills & Boon Limited

© Alex Ryder 1995

Australian copyright 1995   Philippine copyright 1995 This edition 1995

ISBN 0 263 78900 4

Set in Times Roman 10½ on 12 pt. 01-9503-51863 C

Made and printed in Great Britain

CHAPTER ONE

AVALON swore under her breath, then clenched her fists and bit her lip in anger. It had happened again! How was it possible? You'd have thought that just for once Fate might have given her a break instead of dropping her in the sludge yet again. You'd have thought that just for once it might have left her to get on with her life in peace. What did it have against her, for heaven's sake? She was kind to animals and she always gave up her seat in the bus to older people or young mums with kids. But no. Someone up there really seemed to have it in for her. And this time it wasn't just your common-or-garden-type disaster. She was used to coping with them. This time it was mind-blowingly serious. When someone poked a gun into your ribs and snarled, 'I'll deal with you later,' then pushed you into your cabin and locked the door, you were entitled to break into a cold sweat.

She shivered with apprehension, then took a deep, steadying breath. One thing was for sure. Panic wouldn't get her anywhere. If she was going to get out of this mess in one piece she'd have to keep her wits about her.

The cabin was tiny and too cramped to pace back and forward so she sat down on her bunk, her green eyes flickering with anger. She'd had a bad feeling about this job right from the start and she should have trusted her instincts. There had been something about Mr Smith and his partner—not to mention their 'wives'—that hadn't rung true, but at the time she'd been desperate enough to put her suspicions aside and jump at the chance of working her passage back to England. Anyway, when you were stranded in a foreign country with no money, no passport and no-where to sleep, your options were pretty limited.

She'd warned them that she was no cordon bleu cook but Mr Smith had assured her that all that would be required of her was plain, simple fare. As long as she could scramble eggs and grill an occasional steak they'd be satisfied.

The lying toad, she thought bitterly. They hadn't wanted a cook. They'd hired her to be a scapegoat in case anything had gone wrong with their plan and now that she'd found out what they were really up to they were going to make damned sure that she never got the chance to go to the police. They were probably going to dump her overboard when they were far enough away from the coast.

From their point of view it couldn't have been simpler. Her job was done. No one but they knew that she was aboard this motor-cruiser and if she mys-teriously disappeared off the face of the earth there was no way they could be connected with the affair. Anyway, who would miss her enough to make en-quiries? Not one single soul that she could think of.

Well, either she could sit here moaning and getting more terrified by the minute as she waited for Mr Smith to return or she could do something about it. Getting resolutely to her feet, she leaned over the bunk and peered through the porthole. It was almost dark but she could see the even darker mass of a coastline barely a quarter of a mile away. Where were they, anyway? It had been five days since they'd left Portugal. Surely they must be near England by now?

The porthole wasn't very big, but then neither was she. It would be a tight squeeze but she reckoned she could make it. The cabin was right at the stern of the boat, so unless anyone happened to be looking back from the bridge she should be able to get away without being spotted. She was a fairly good swimmer and the sea didn't appear to be too rough.

If only there were a sign of habitation ashore. A light from a house. Anything. She'd have to get in touch with the authorities and she couldn't do that if she ended up on some deserted little island. If that happened she'd either die of starvation or exposure.

Suddenly she blinked, and rubbed her eyes and stared towards the land. There! There it was again! A bluish-white light flickering—like a huge candle-flame. It died away but her heart had already given a wild beat of hope. A light meant people... civilisation!

Realising that it was now or never, she quickly unscrewed the brass butterfly nuts and opened the glass cover, then put her arms and head through the opening. Once her shoulders were through she turned awkwardly on her back and reached up. Her scrabbling fingers found the edge of the deck and she pulled and hoisted the rest of her body through the porthole. For a ghastly moment her slim hips got firmly wedged and she could neither get out nor go back in. She kept squirming and struggling and bruising her skin against the hard edges then, like a cork out of a bottle, she popped free.

Six feet beneath her the dark, oily-looking water slid by and she could see the frothy wake astern of

the ship. She was in a crouching position, her toes on
the bottom lip of the porthole and her fingertips desperately clinging to the deck above. The big danger
now was the propellers. She'd have to jump far enough
backwards to be clear of them. Raising herself higher,
she took a quick look forward towards the bridge to
make sure that no one was looking astern then, taking
a deep breath, she pushed with her legs and launched
herself into space.

The shock as she hit the water drove the breath from
her body and she fought and struggled her way to the
surface, choking and gasping for air. My God! It was
absolutely freezing! Where was she? Iceland? Her
teeth began chattering and as she rose on a heavy swell
she saw the stern light of the cruiser disappearing into
the night.

At that moment she was far too concerned with her
ability to survive in this icy water to feel any sense of
triumph at her escape, and in desperation she struck
out for the shore. After a few yards she trod water
and kicked off her sandals. It would be better to reach
land barefooted than not reach it at all.

A spasm of cramp gripped her thigh muscles and
she almost sobbed in despair. The sense of feeling was
leaving her fingers and toes and she knew that the
numbness would gradually creep all over her until she
no longer felt anything. At that point she'd get drowsy
and simply give up. It would be the end of everything.

Slowly she drew nearer to the shore and she heard
the rumble of the surf dashing against the rocks. Her
strength was ebbing fast and she no longer had the
energy to swim. She was completely at the mercy of
the elements now. She closed her eyes, sobbed
and prayed.

The tide swept her relentlessly towards the shore then one wave, larger than the others, bore her high in the air then tossed her carelessly on to a large slab of granite. The receding water surged around her inert body and she felt a sharp pain in her head—and then . . . nothing.

The dream came later. There was a sensation of floating on a warm, soft cloud and from a great distance she heard a woman's voice saying, 'I told you she was coming, didn't I? From the sea, just like the others. The legend has come true after all.'

'You say that old Gavin found her?' That was a man's voice. Deeply resonant. A voice used to command and demanding respect.

'Aye. On the rocks just past the point.'

'But where did she come from?'

'Does that matter?'

'Of course it matters, woman. The legend may or may not be true. I'm going to need a lot more evidence than this. Her eyes are half-open. Have you tried talking to her?'

'It's concussion. She can't see or hear anything. All she needs is a good night's rest and she'll be as right as rain in the morning—apart from a sore head.'

The man didn't sound too convinced. 'You're sure there are no other injuries? Nothing broken?'

'Positive. Have a look for yourself.'

It was a good job it was only a dream, Avalon told herself. The top cover was whisked away, leaving her lying naked on the bed. Then the man's voice became a face. The shape hovering over her was blurred and indistinct but she had an impression of raven-black hair and piercing blue eyes. Then his hands were exploring her body. She should have told him to stop being so familiar but her limbs seemed to be filled with warm honey and she couldn't even murmur. Besides . . . there was something exciting about his touch.

Finally he stood up but continued to stare down at her. 'She's young,' he remarked. 'Eighteen or nineteen.'

'And a right pretty wee thing, Fraser. Look at that fine blonde silvery hair and the lovely green eyes. Just like a sea nymph. She'll make a bonnie bride, I'm thinking.'

'Aye . . .' the voice replied gruffly. 'But I need to know more about her.'

'She's perfect, I tell you. They wouldn't have sent her otherwise.'

'Well, perhaps you're right and perhaps not. We'll have to wait until she wakes up, then we'll get to the truth of the matter.'

Avalon tried to smile up at him and tell him that she came from London but she was too tired, and slowly the faces and voices disappeared as she slid back into the darkness of her mind.

When she awoke she blinked in the sunlight streaming through the window. For a moment she lay, staring around the strange room, wondering where she was, then the memories rushed back and a shiver of fear ran through her body as she recalled her ordeal in the sea. The porthole . . . The plunge into the icy water. . . The roar of the surf dashing against the rocks. She wondered now how she'd ever had the nerve to go through with such a thing. By some miracle she'd been saved and brought here.

She struggled to sit up, then groaned as a heavy band of steel seemed to tighten viciously round her head. Cautiously, she raised her hand and felt the bump on her temple.

She opened her eyes again slowly and took in her surroundings. The room was simply furnished—just the bed she was on, a dressing-table and a chair. The walls, like the ceiling, were bare and whitewashed and the only touch of colour about the place was provided by a huge jar of wild flowers on the windowsill. The floor was pine, deeply glossed through years of polishing, and boasting a huge sheepskin rug by the bedside. There was no sign of her clothes, however, and she had no intention of walking around naked looking for them.

A faint sound from beyond the door caught her attention and she cried out. 'Hello? Hello? Anyone at home?'

An instant later the door opened and a woman poked her head round. 'Well, well! So you're awake at last.' She opened the door wider and came in. 'And none the worse for wear by the look of you.'

She was a stout, amiable old dear with iron-grey hair and button-bright eyes the colour of hazelnuts. Her ample figure bulged beneath a chunky sweater and she wore thick stockings beneath a tweed skirt. Motherly was the description that sprang to Avalon's mind.

From the bed she smiled up uncertainly. 'Hello... How did I...?'

The woman raised a hand. 'Just you wait till I put the kettle on. You'll feel much better after a cup of tea.'

As she left the room Avalon looked at the closed door thoughtfully. The woman's voice had sounded vaguely familiar. She recalled a dream. Or had it been

a dream? There had also been a man... Tall...dark...
Her frown deepened as she tried to remember the details, then she gave up.

There was one thing she did remember only too
damn well, though. Mr Smith's threat to deal with
her later. They were bound to have discovered about
her escape by now. What would they be doing about
it? Well, they might think that she'd drowned—but
could they take that chance? In all probability they'd
have turned round and would be at this very moment
trying to find out if she'd managed to get ashore
somewhere.

The first thing she had to do was to notify the local
police and let them deal with Mr Smith and his friends.
Impatiently she got out of bed and stared through the
window. The house seemed to be built on a slight rise
but the view, from this window at least, consisted of
nothing more than miles of empty, desolate moorland
stretching into a purple, hazy distance. It was like no
land Avalon had ever seen before and she wondered
where she was. The woman's accent had been oddly
soft and lilting, yet it hadn't sounded Irish. Scotland,
then? Some place on the west coast of Scotland?
Thoughtfully she climbed back into bed. All right. So
she was stranded in some Godforsaken spot in the
wilds of Scotland and she didn't have a penny to her
name nor a pair of shoes to her feet. But at least she
was still alive.

The woman bustled in a few minutes later with a
mug of hot, sweet tea. 'Now, just stay there and drink
this. And here's an old dressing-gown and a pair of
slippers to wear until I've finished drying and ironing
your clothes. When you've finished your tea you can

have a nice hot bath. We must have you looking your best when the Chief arrives.'

Avalon looked at her with a blank expression. 'Chief? Chief of what?'

'Of the Clan, of course. Young Fraser of Suilvach. Lord of the Deer and Eagles, to give him his correct title.' She paused. 'By the way, you seem to have lost your shoes. I'll phone the harbour store and have them send up a pair of plimsolls. What size do you take?'

Avalon's mouth had been hanging open and now she got her wits back. 'Er... size four. And thanks, Mrs...er...?'

The woman gave a hearty chuckle. 'My name is Kirsty. And it's Miss. Can't you tell an old maid when you see one?'

'Well... you're being very kind, Kirsty. My name is Avalon.'

'Yes. I know.'

Her mouth dropped open again. 'You know?'

'Of course. They told me your name. And they described you perfectly.'

A knot of fear settled in Avalon's chest. 'They? Has... has there been anyone asking about me? A stranger calling himself Mr Smith?'

Kirsty frowned, then shook her head. 'There's no one called Smith around here. And definitely no strangers.' She smiled benevolently. 'Don't you bother yourself about folk asking questions. You're perfectly safe here. You've nothing to worry about.'

Nothing to worry about? That's all she knew, Avalon told herself wryly. 'Is... is there a police station near here?' she asked hopefully.

For the merest second Kirsty's smile lost some of its warmth, then she scoffed, 'The nearest police station is in Oban and that's over four hours by boat. We don't need the police here. We've always managed without them. What happens here is our business and no one else's.'

Avalon's spirits sank. Four hours by boat! This place must be even more remote than she'd thought. 'You mentioned a harbour,' she persisted. 'Is it far from here?'

'Put on that dressing-gown and I'll show it to you,' offered Kirsty.

A few moments later they were standing at the front door of the cottage. From here there was a commanding view over the fair-sized fishing village. Nestled in a sheltered bay the white-painted houses and buildings looked clean and well-looked-after. A few brightly painted fishing boats were tied up at the jetty in the sleepy-looking harbour but there was nothing remotely resembling a motor-cruiser.

Avalon breathed a silent sigh of relief. She was safe for the moment, at least.

'What do you think?' asked Kirsty at her elbow. 'Pretty little place, isn't it?'

Avalon wasn't yet in the mood to appreciate the finer points of the scenery but she murmured politely, 'It's lovely. Very picturesque. What's it called?'

'Port Suilvach.' Kirsty pointed across the bay to an imposing, granite-built mansion, half hidden behind a stand of pine trees. 'That's the Chief's house. You'll be staying there from now on.' She paused for a moment, then added, 'I really expected you sooner, but better late than never, I suppose.'

Avalon eyed her uncertainly. There was something decidedly odd going on here. Or perhaps it was just

Kirsty. She was pleasant enough but seemed a bit eccentric.

They went back inside the cottage and Avalon had a chance to look around. Although there was an atmosphere of solid comfort she had the peculiar feeling that she'd entered some sort of time-warp. A fire burned brightly in an ancient blackleaded grate that apparently served for cooking and heating water as well as providing warmth. An old Victorian sideboard surmounted by silver-framed photographs and two blue and white china dogs took up most of one side of the room while a sombre-looking grandfather clock stood in the corner, reluctantly ticking off the seconds.

'Bacon and eggs suit you?' Kirsty asked cheerfully.

Avalon, feeling lost and rather foolish standing there in her grossly oversized slippers and dressing-gown, nodded and admitted quietly that she felt as if she hadn't eaten for a week.

Kirsty beamed. 'A healthy appetite is a good sign. Well, the bathroom is through that door. By the time you've had your bath I'll have your breakfast ready.'

The bath was a cast-iron and chipped enamel museum piece, but as Avalon relaxed in the hot sudsy water she wasn't inclined to be critical. She had far too much to be thankful for—not least the fact that she was being offered such overwhelming hospitality by a complete stranger.

More relaxed now, Avalon considered her next move. Perhaps she should just try to forget all about Mr Smith and his friends and put it down to experience. No doubt the law would catch up with him sooner or later. She definitely didn't want to see or get involved with them again, and if she reported them to the police she'd end up having to go to court and answer a lot of damned awkward questions. Once she got back to London she'd simply fade anonymously into the population and try to start a new life.

Half an hour later, pink and glowing and feeling at least halfway civilised in her own freshly laundered clothes, she sat at the plain deal table and pushed her empty plate away. 'That was delicious, Kirsty. I've never enjoyed a breakfast as much as that.'

Kirsty chuckled. 'Aye. I could tell by the way you were tucking in.' She produced a battered tin full of dark tobacco and deftly rolled herself a cigarette then, after tapping it expertly on her thumb, lit it and blew an acrid cloud of smoke at the ceiling. 'I don't suppose folk from London ever bother to bake their own bread. And of course the eggs come from my own hens out the back and the butter is fresh-made in the village creamery. And the water here isn't full of chemicals. Oh, aye, you'll find a big difference living here in Port Suilvach.'

It was on the tip of Avalon's tongue to tell her that she'd no intention of staying here any longer than she could help when there was a loud rap at the front door and her heart gave a lurch. Could that be Mr Smith—or one of his gang—searching for her?

Kirsty gave her an odd look followed by a re-assuring smile, then called out loudly, 'Come in, Jamie.'

A tousled, red-haired, freckle-faced eight-year-old burst in and handed Avalon a shoebox along with a torrent of Gaelic and only stopped when Kirsty re-proved him gently. 'Mind your manners, Jamie. Avalon doesn't have the Gaelic yet. You must talk to her in English.'

The boy flushed, grinned, then said breathlessly, 'You have to try them on and if they don't fit I've to take them back and get them changed and is there anything else you need?'

They were top-of-the-range trainers. Avalon tried them on, then smiled at the boy. 'They're perfect, Jamie. And no, there's nothing else I need at the moment.'

As soon as he'd gone Avalon poured another two cups of tea from the enormous teapot. 'We'll have this then I'll help you with the washing-up,' she offered. 'Then I'll have to go down to the village. Do you think there's any chance of me finding a few days' work there?'

The brown eyes widened in shocked surprise. 'Work? But . . . why?'

'Why?' Avalon repeated. 'Because I've no money, that's why. I'll have to earn enough to repay you for all this and then pay my fare home. Of course I suppose I could always hitch-hike. That would save——'

'Oh, you poor wee thing!' Kirsty burst out suddenly. 'I . . . I didn't realise. You still haven't any idea why you were brought here. How could you? You must have been wondering what I was talking about half the time.'

'Well . . .' said Avalon, feeling thoroughly bemused at Kirsty's outburst. 'I'm sorry, Kirsty, but at the risk of appearing rude I still don't know what you're talking about. No one brought me here. It was just— just an accident.'

'You may think it was an accident but it was all planned by them,' Kirsty maintained stoutly. 'They

told me. How else do you think I knew your name
or that you came from London?'

She could see that Kirsty was beginning to get agitated and she replied in a calm, reasonable voice.
'Well, anyone can tell from my accent that I come
from London. And, as for my name... Well, perhaps
you heard me talking in my sleep last night. That's
the most likely explanation, isn't it?'

Kirsty gave an emphatic shake to her head. 'You
must believe me, Avalon. The guardians brought you
here to us. Your destiny is here.'

Oh, God, thought Avalon. She'd been right. There
definitely was something odd about Kirsty.
Guardians... and destiny? Mild delusions, more likely.
Perhaps she'd been living here too long on her own.
There was probably a medical name for it.

Kirsty heaved a sigh. 'Oh, dear. I suppose the
sooner you know the truth the better.'

Avalon gave her a cautious smile. You didn't argue
in cases like this. You simply played along and pretended to agree with everything they said.

'I've known about you coming here for the last two
months,' Kirsty began quietly. 'The guardians told me
to expect you. They assured me that the old tradition
would carry on.'

'And what tradition is that?' Avalon asked with
feigned interest.

'The bride of the Clan Chief always comes from
the sea.' Kirsty took another puff at her cigarette. 'You
can't deny that you came from the sea, can you?'

Somehow, Avalon managed not to laugh outright.
'No. You're right about that. So you're telling me that
I was brought here to marry this . . . this . . . What was
his name again?'

Kirsty eyed her solemnly. 'Young Fraser of Suilvach. Soon you'll be his wife and the First Lady of the Clan.'

'Well, that's nice,' said Avalon, going on with the game. 'I'm sure that it's a great honour, Kirsty, but are you sure that your Chief will agree to marry a complete stranger?'

Kirsty gave an emphatic nod. 'He'll marry you gladly. You've been chosen by the guardians, you see. If he were to refuse their choice... Well, it would bring nothing but disaster to the Clan. We don't want that, do we?'

'No,' Avalon agreed in a grave voice, 'we certainly don't.' If she ever told anyone about this they'd laugh in her face and accuse her of making it up. 'Look,' she said in quiet desperation, 'these Clan guardians you keep talking about. Are they a committee or something? If they're down in the village perhaps I can go and have a chat with them. We can get all this sorted out without anyone getting into trouble.'

Kirsty laughed at the very idea. 'The guardians don't live in the village. They live on the Nevay.'

Avalon held her patience. 'All right, then. Where's the Nevay? Is it far from here?'

'Not at all. You can see it from the bedroom window.'

Avalon thought for a moment. 'When I looked out of the window I couldn't see a thing. Just empty moorland stretching for miles.'

'Aye,' nodded Kirsty. 'That's the Nevay. The enchanted land. That's where they live.'

The enchanted land? Suddenly Avalon was seized by a horrible suspicion and she took a deep breath.

'Kirsty? Who exactly are these guardians? What do they look like? Can you describe them to me?'

Kirsty laughed again. 'Good heavens, lassie! No one has ever seen the guardians. They like to be left alone. They're shy. And apart from that they don't really trust us mere mortals. They think we're coarse and ignorant. I'm the only one around here they ever talk to. Whenever they have something to tell me they send me a sign. Sometimes it's a light at night and I go out to the Nevay and listen to their voices.'

An unaccountable shiver ran down Avalon's spine and the words were out before she realised what she was saying. 'I saw a light last night. A big, tall flame. That's how I knew someone was here.'

Kirsty nodded wisely. 'That was the Fire Magic. If you saw it then that proves you were the one who was chosen.'

Avalon stared at her in amazement, her suspicions now a certainty. This perfectly normal-looking nice old lady was telling her that she'd been brought here by fairies to marry a Clan Chief! Some big, hairy ruffian in a kilt, no doubt. It was unbelievable! Fairies . . . ? God almighty!

Weakly, she got to her feet and managed a smile. 'You just sit there and rest, Kirsty. I'll do the washing-up.'

'Aye,' Kirsty said cheerfully. 'And then I'll give you a brush and you can do something with your hair. We can't have the Chief seeing you like that, can we?'

CHAPTER TWO

NEITHER of them had heard the Land Rover drawing up outside. Avalon had just finished brushing the tangles out of her long, silvery blonde hair and was surveying the result critically in the mirror when she saw the reflection of the man striding through the door. She turned slowly, then stiffened and felt a hot flush of resentment rush to her cheeks. So last night it hadn't been a dream after all. This was the same raven-haired man who'd gazed down at her on the bed and run his hands over her naked body.

Over six feet tall and wide-shouldered, he seemed to fill the room with his sheer dominating presence. In her 'dream' last night his features had been blurred and indistinct but now every detail imprinted itself on her mind—the finely chiselled nose and cheekbones, and the wide sensual mouth. Every uncompromising line added up to a display of proud, almost arrogant power and self-assurance. His clothes sat easily on his lean, muscular body—a plaid shirt rolled up at the sleeves and light brown cords tucked into hard-worn combat boots. And those eyes! They were fixed on her now like two blue lasers scorching their way through the tattered fabric of her dignity.

Finally he spoke in a hard, clipped voice. 'I'm Fraser of Suilvach. I hear that you're the girl I'm supposed to take as my wife.'

Oh, my God! She'd been hoping that when he arrived he'd simply take her down to the village, apologise for Kirsty's strange delusions and send her on her merry way, but now it was obvious that she had another crank on her hands. Well, enough was enough. She didn't mind humouring Kirsty but she was damned if she'd play this game with him. She decided simply to ignore him, then had second thoughts. There was a dangerous, hard edge to this man and she guessed that people ignored him at their peril.

Impatient for an answer, he turned to Kirsty. 'Has our little sea-witch eaten yet?'

Kirsty nodded happily. 'Aye. There's nothing wrong with her appetite.'

'And does she have a name?'

'It's Avalon. I said it would be, didn't I?'

'Yes, Kirsty. You did.' His blue eyes returned to Avalon and began surveying her doubtfully from head to toe, like a man deciding whether or not to buy a second-hand car. Finally he growled, 'She's pretty enough, I grant you that. Are you quite sure that she's the one?'

Kirsty was busy rolling herself another cigarette. She licked the paper then bobbed her head. 'There can't be any doubt about it now, Fraser. Didn't she just tell me herself that it was the Fire Magic that guided her here?'

Avalon groaned and began to sink into a morass of despair. Fairies! Fire Magic! This was like something from *The Twilight Zone*. Were they all crazy up here? God knew what kind of things they got up to at the full moon. Painted themselves blue and howled at the sky?

Suddenly she flinched and drew away as he reached out to touch her face, and he rapped, 'Stand still, dammit. I want to see that bruise on your temple.'

Anger at last overrode her caution and she snapped back at him, 'My bruises have nothing to do with you. Kindly keep your hands to yourself. I don't like being treated like some circus freak.'

There was a tense, crackling silence then Kirsty said placatingly, 'The poor wee thing is still a bit confused, Fraser. She'll need time to settle down.'

'Aye,' he observed grimly. 'And she'll have to learn some manners while she's at it. When I ask a question I expect the courtesy of a reply. Perhaps you should go and tell your friends on the Nevay that I've no intention of saddling myself with a woman I know nothing about but who seems to be as cold as the sea that gave her birth.'

The threat obviously alarmed Kirsty and she hastened to reassure him again. 'She's a lovely little creature, Fraser. Just give her time. All this must be very strange to her.'

The Clan Chief didn't seem the least bit moved by this desperate appeal to his patience. Glowering beneath his dark brows, he observed drily, 'I'm getting the feeling that our green-eyed little mermaid thinks we're a couple of fools.' He continued to stare at Avalon in an unnerving silence which turned her mouth dry with apprehension, then he questioned her sharply. 'I want to know how you got yourself washed up on my property last night like a piece of wreckage.'

She was tempted to tell him to go and ask the fairies but thought better of it. He was liable to bite her head off. 'I was on a boat,' she muttered. 'I . . . I fell overboard and swam ashore.'

He raised a darkly mocking brow. 'You fell over-board? That was a damned clumsy thing to do. What kind of boat was it?'

She eyed him truculently. 'A motor-cruiser.'

'How many people were on board?'

She sighed. 'Five. Including me.'

'And none of them saw this . . . accident happen?'

'No.' She avoided his eye. 'It was dark and I was the only one on deck.'

'Well, no doubt they've discovered your absence by now so presumably they'll be reporting the incident to the authorities.'

She bit her lip and kept avoiding his eye. 'Yes. I suppose so.'

He subjected her to another silent scrutiny then he turned towards the door and gestured for her to follow. 'Right. Let's go.'

His cold, overbearing manner refuelled her anger and she entertained the notion of telling him to go to hell, but once again the danger of the situation she was in demanded caution. If she refused he wouldn't think twice about slinging her over his shoulder. Until she found some way of getting back to civilisation and out of his clutches she'd no option but to put up with his tyrannical behaviour.

'Fraser! Wait.'

He turned in the doorway. 'Yes, Kirsty?'

The older woman looked worried. 'Be good to her, Fraser. Promise me you'll look after her. Until the Grand Ceilidh, at least.'

He sighed heavily. 'You know what my plans are for the Grand Ceilidh.'

'Aye. But plans can be changed. My...my friends don't want Pamela here. That's why they've sent Avalon. Please be kind to her.'

The Clan Chief eyed her sternly, then he relented. 'All right, for your sake, Kirsty, I'll see that she comes to no harm. She'll stay with me until the ball and we'll see what happens.'

Kirsty smiled with relief and Avalon desperately weighed up the chances of making a mad dash for freedom. Anywhere back in the land of reality would do.

As the Land Rover set off along the track she looked at him suspiciously. 'Where are you taking me? I thought we were going to the village.'

He ignored her question. 'How did you manage to fall overboard? The sea wasn't rough last night.'

'I...I tripped over a rope,' she lied. 'I told you. It was dark.' She knew there was no use telling him the truth. He wouldn't believe her. No one would.

The Land Rover was bucketing recklessly along the rough, potholed track that skirted the shore and rounded the headland to the south. She clung to her seat grimly and wished the maniac would slow down.

'What was the name of the boat you were on?' he shouted, apparently determined to go on with his relentless questioning.

'*C-C-Caprice*,' she told him through chattering teeth.

'Where was it heading for?'

She glared at him in a temper and raised her voice over the noise of the engine and the rumble of the wheels. 'I've no idea. And I can't carry on a conversation while I'm being rattled about like this.'

He glanced at her sideways and made no comment,
and as soon as his eyes were back on the road she
made a face and stuck her tongue out at him. She had
to endure another five minutes of the torturous
journey then he slammed on the brakes, killed the
engine, and got out.

She remained still, her arms folded and her eyes
fixed straight ahead. He got out, then went round and
opened her door. 'Get out.' To her surprise he actually helped her down to the ground. She looked
around nervously, wondering what he had in mind
for her now. On her left there was nothing but that
barren, windswept moor while to her right the ground
fell sharply down to the rocky coastline.

'Why did you stop here?' she demanded
suspiciously.

'This is where you were found last night.' He
pointed down to the black barnacled rocks. 'Lying
down there. Half-frozen and unconscious.' He paused,
then added quietly, 'You're an extremely lucky young
lady. Old Gavin MacLean was driving by in his tractor
and if he hadn't looked down and spotted you you'd
certainly have died from exposure.'

She tore her gaze away from the rocks and said
humbly, 'Yes. You're right. If I ever see him I'll thank
him.'

'You'll see him,' he assured her with an ironic smile.
'In the meantime you can answer a few questions.'

'I'm sorry,' she said firmly. 'I don't feel like
answering any more questions. I don't see what right
you've got to subject me to this kind of——'

'I've got every right in the world. You're not in
London now. You're on my property,' he reminded
her harshly. 'Technically speaking you're a trespasser

and I could prosecute you. So while you're here you will do as you're told and you'll answer any damned question I feel like asking. Is that clear?'

She gulped. He was like a wolf baring its fangs and she hurried to placate him. 'All right. Calm down. What do you want to know?'

He gave a satisfied nod and permitted something vaguely resembling a cold smile to flit across his face. 'That's better. Now, we'll start off with your full name.'

'Avalon Rivers,' she replied stiffly.

'How old are you?'

'Nineteen.'

'Parents? Where do they live?'

She sniffed and knew she was going to catch a cold. 'I don't have any.' She saw him frown and she explained patiently, 'I never knew them. I was raised in an orphanage. As far as I know they were killed in a car accident when I was a year old.'

'I'm sorry to hear it,' he said quietly.

'There's no need to be,' she assured him tartly. 'It has nothing to do with you.'

His face hardened again. 'How about friends? Any close friends?'

A chill wind had sprung up, sending low grey clouds scurrying in from the sea. 'Only acquaintances.'

'What about boyfriends?' he demanded.

She shook her head.

'Hmmm...' He gave her a long, sceptical look. 'An attractive young girl like you without a boyfriend? That's hard to believe.'

'And I'm finding all this hard to believe,' she flared in sudden resentment. 'If you must know, I had a boyfriend but it's all over. We had an argument and

I told him that he was nothing but a snake and I walked out on him.'

He raised his brows in cold amusement. 'That sounds interesting. Tell me about it.'

She glared at him, then sighed. 'Listen . . . Is all this really necessary?' The deep growl from his throat decided her that it was and she explained hastily, 'We worked for the same company. I got an idea for processing the paperwork more efficiently and I told him about it. That very same day he took my idea to one of the directors and pretended it was his. It ended up with him getting the credit and the promotion. Needless to say I told him what I thought of him and walked out in disgust.'

He shook his head. 'That was stupid. You should have stayed and waited for your chance to get even.'

Yes, she felt like saying. But we're not all as cold-blooded as you, are we?

'Did you ever sleep with him or are you still a virgin?'

The bluntness of his question rocked her and her face went red. 'That's none of your damn business.'

He growled like an angry bear again. 'I'm making it my business. You'd better give me an answer or I'll find out for myself right here and now.'

She glared back at him but the defiance in her eyes turned to horror as he begun unbuckling the belt around his waist. Backing away from him, she gasped, 'You . . . you wouldn't dare.' But as soon as she'd said the words she knew that she was wrong. This cretin was ruthless enough to do anything. This was his land and he was the lord and master here. Even if there had been anyone around to hear her screaming for help, they'd make sure to keep well out of the way.

'I—I've never slept with any man,' she said breathlessly. 'That's the honest truth. I swear it. Now, don't you dare touch me.'

He eyed her darkly for a moment then reluctantly he fastened his belt. 'It had better be the truth,' he warned her. 'Because if I do decide to take you as my wife and I find out on our wedding night that you've been lying to me you'll live to regret it.'

'Well, you've got no worries on that score,' she grated. 'I've no intention of marrying you. In fact, if you were the only man left on this planet I'd stay as far away from you as possible. You're the most detestable, arrogant——'

'I don't think you've got any choice in the matter, Miss Rivers,' he broke in coldly. 'Your fate is entirely in my hands and you're going to stay here until I've made up my mind whether you're worthy or not to become First Lady of this Clan.'

She put her hands on her hips, tossed her head and scoffed at him, 'Is that a fact? And what's to stop me leaving here right now? If I walk far enough I'll be bound to reach a main road and get a lift south. Or perhaps you're hoping that your fairies will turn me into a frog or something?'

A thin smile twisted his lips. 'Nothing quite as drastic as that. But it's forty miles of single-track road before you'd ever have a chance of getting a lift. Perhaps two cars a week use the road out of here. The only other way is by boat and since I own all the boats here I merely have to give orders that you're not to be allowed aboard in any circumstances.'

Filled with a sense of outrage, she spluttered at him, 'You can't do that! You can't keep me here a prisoner against my will!'

His blue eyes mocked her. 'I can do anything I like with you, my dear girl,' he said softly. 'Who's going to stop me? Your friends from the *Caprice*?' He saw her bite her lip and he laughed. 'I don't think we need worry about them coming here. Anyway, we'll talk about them later. At the moment it's you I'm interested in.'

She shivered and looked at him helplessly. 'Look— I'm freezing. Are we going to stand here all day?'

'Yes, if necessary.' He leaned into the Land Rover, then took out a travelling-rug and handed it to her. 'Put this around your shoulders.'

She wrapped herself up then wondered if it would do any good appealing to his better nature—always assuming that he had such a thing. 'Look,' she said quietly, 'there isn't any sense in this, is there? If you want a wife why don't you choose a local girl? I mean—apart from needing a personality transplant— I'm sure most women find you attractive. But you and I? We don't even like each other, do we? And please don't give me all that rubbish about legends and magic fires and fairies. I wasn't born yesterday.'

The blue eyes measured her coldly, sending another shiver through her in spite of the rug around her shoulders. 'Kirsty is the one who believes in fairies,' he snapped. 'I believe in hard facts. Nevertheless, I respect Kirsty. Everyone here does. That's why I've promised her that I'll look after you.'

'Until you've made up your mind whether I'm worth marrying or not,' she observed drily. 'My feelings don't even matter to you, do they?'

'You've only got yourself to blame for the position you're in,' he said coldly. 'No one invited you here. I've got better things to do than play nursemaid to a

bad-tempered little teenager. Your presence here is
going to cause me considerable problems.'

'Well, I'm sorry. If I'd known I was going to be all
this trouble I'd have just let myself drown instead of
swimming.'

He ignored her sarcasm. 'One fact I can't ignore is
that Kirsty seems to like you. Whatever it is she sees
in you eludes me for the moment, but I'm going to
find out.'

She challenged him again, indignantly. 'I'm sure
there are plenty of women here who'd jump at the
chance of being your wife. Why pick on me? I'm entitled to know that, at least.'

'You're still a stranger,' he told her bluntly. 'All a
stranger is entitled to here is food, shelter and hospitality—which you've been given.'

She glared at him in silent exasperation, then tried
a new idea. 'I don't know anything about you, this
part of the country, or the people. I wouldn't fit in
here and I'm certainly not worthy enough to be the
First Lady of anything. I was shunted from one foster
home to another when I was a kid. I've got no
breeding whatsoever. You're just wasting your time
with me.'

Those damned eyes of his mocked her again and
he growled, 'Aye. I suspect you're right. But I'm the
one who decides, not you. So from now on, Miss
Rivers, you'll answer my questions without resorting
to lies or evasion. Is that clear?'

'I'm not in the habit of telling lies,' she retorted
angrily. 'And I object to the way you——'

His voice cut through her protestation like a blade
of cold steel. 'Like you, I wasn't born yesterday. If a
boat has only got five crew and one of them suddenly

disappears the others are bound to notice sooner or later, wouldn't you agree? First thing this morning I contacted the nearest coastguard station to find out if any ship had reported a missing crew member. Well, no such report had been made. How do you account for that, Miss Rivers?'

'Perhaps they...they haven't got round to reporting it yet,' she said evasively.

Suddenly her shoulder was grabbed in a vice-like grip and he thrust his face closer to hers. 'They didn't make any report because they didn't want to draw attention to themselves. That's the truth, isn't it, Miss Rivers?'

She ran her tongue nervously over her lips. The man's anger was like an icy blast from the polar wastes, chilling her to the marrow. 'L—look,' she stammered. 'I—I——'

'Save your breath,' he grated. 'Two hours after you were found on this beach last night a motor-cruiser called *Caprice* tied up at a deserted pier fifteen miles north of here. The police and Customs were waiting and your friends are now in custody.'

Her feeling of relief that Smith and his confederates had been caught was short-lived at the realisation that she was now being accused of being part of the gang. In wide-eyed consternation she blurted, 'You...you've got it all wrong.'

'Have I?' he asked, with harsh scepticism. 'By your own admission you were a member of the crew. And if you hadn't ''accidentally'' fallen overboard you, too, would be in custody.'

She winced at the pressure of his hand. 'Let go my shoulder, damn you. You're hurting me.'

When he let her go she glared up at him. 'All right! So I did lie to you. But I was just the cook on that damned boat. I didn't know what they were up to. And I didn't fall overboard. I jumped.' She paused and gave a bitter sigh. 'It's a long story and you probably wouldn't believe a word of it, anyway.'

He studied her shrewdly, then growled, 'I might. But no more lies. Understand? If you aren't part of that gang then what were you doing on the boat in the first place?'

'I told you,' she muttered. 'I was just the cook.'

'So you say,' he derided. 'But you'll have to do better than that.'

'Dammit! I'm telling you the truth.'

'How long had you been working for them?'

She sighed. 'Only a few days. I met them in Portugal. My hotel room——'

'What were you doing in Portugal?'

It was obvious that he wasn't going to be satisfied until he'd wrung every last detail from her so she began again. 'After the row with my ex-boyfriend I quit my job and decided to take a holiday.'

'To mend your broken heart, no doubt.'

She ignored the sarcastic interruption and went on. 'I drew all my savings from the bank, locked up my flat and caught the first available plane. Anyway, I spent the next two weeks swimming and lazing around on the beach and vowing that no man would ever use me or make a fool of me again.' She paused and eyed him bitterly. 'Of course I was wrong, as usual, wasn't I?'

His face was unreadable and she continued reluctantly, 'It was the day before I was due to come home when someone broke into my hotel apartment and I lost everything. Money, passport, clothes . . .'

She had hardly been able to believe her eyes at first when she'd seen the empty drawers and overturned mattress. She'd only been gone for ten minutes and her room had been ransacked! Whoever had done it must have climbed up on to the balcony and entered through the open window.

In a fury she had run downstairs to the reception desk and reported the break-in to the manager.

He was sympathetic but adamant that she had no claim against the hotel. 'Madam should have made sure that the window was securely latched before she went out,' he said. They would inform the police, of course, but there was little hope of catching the culprit and recovering her property. Surely madam had taken out insurance against this sort of thing happening?

Madam hadn't, and she turned from the desk in dismay. With the loose change in her pocket she had barely enough left to buy lunch. And how was she going to get home tomorrow without a plane ticket? She couldn't even think of anyone in London who could forward her a loan. With her spirits at zero she made her way outside and stood on the broad tree-lined pavement completely at a loss as to what to do now.

'They weren't much help, were they? I couldn't help overhearing.'

She turned at the sound of the voice and looked at the middle-aged man who'd followed her out. Instinctively on her guard, she took in his appearance. He seemed harmless enough, but you never could tell. At least he was well-dressed and groomed. The typical English gentleman abroad. Dark blazer

and flannels and some sort of regimental tie over an
immaculately white shirt. He had a clipped moustache
and a friendly smile on his rather bland face.

'No, they weren't,' she answered at last. 'But it was
my own stupid fault.'

'Damned awkward being stranded in a foreign
country,' he sympathised. He held out his hand. 'I'm
Roger Smith. Here with my wife and a couple of
friends.'

She shook hands and gave him a polite smile.
'Avalon Rivers.'

He looked at her sadly. 'Did they actually take
everything?'

She gave a resigned nod. 'I don't know how I'm
going to get home now. My hotel room is paid for
tonight but tomorrow I'll have to sleep on the beach
then try to get a job somewhere.'

He shook his head doubtfully. 'I think you might
need a work permit. As for sleeping on the beach, I
wouldn't recommend it. Far too many odd-looking
characters going around.' He paused as if he'd had a
sudden inspiration. 'Look here, Miss Rivers... I don't
know if the idea will appeal to you or not but there
is a way I can help you out of your predicament. It's
entirely up to you, of course.'

Experience had taught her to be wary of unsolicited
offers of help. There were usually strings attached.

As if sensing her reluctance he went on quickly, 'The
truth of the matter is that you'd be doing both my
wife and me a great favour. We're sailing back to
England tonight but the girl who was doing our
cooking has decided to stay on. She seems to have
formed some kind of attachment to a local boy and

is quite devastated at the thought of leaving him. Anyway, the position is yours if you want it.'

It sounded almost too good to be true and she said cautiously, 'It's a wonderful offer, Mr Smith, and I'm grateful, but I'm afraid I'm not much of a cook.'

He laughed and brushed her objection aside. 'I admire your honesty, but you've nothing to worry about. We don't go in for *haute cuisine* aboard the *Caprice*. Just plain, simple cooking. I'm sure you can manage that.'

A voice in her head was telling her to be careful. All this seemed like too much of a coincidence to sit comfortably, but she stifled it. She was in danger of becoming a distrustful cynic. Anyway, the offer and Mr Smith seemed genuine enough. If she passed up this chance she'd still be left with the problem of how to get back to England.

'The trip shouldn't take too long,' he went on persuasively. 'And of course I'll see that you're well paid at the end of it.'

That was enough to settle the matter and she smiled at him. 'All right, Mr Smith. When would you like me to start?'

He rubbed his hands together briskly. 'Good show. I'll take you to the boat now and show you around.'

They went by taxi to the harbour where he led her down the gangway on to the deck of a motor-cruiser. She knew nothing about boats but she could tell affluence when she saw it. Beneath the bridge there was a hatchway and once they were down the short flight of steps he proudly showed her the layout. There were two large and luxuriously furnished cabins at the front. The main lounge and dining-room was amidships, and to the rear of that was the galley where the meals were prepared. A door led from the rear of the galley and he pushed it open. 'This will be your own cabin. It's small but I'm sure you'll find it comfortable enough.'

She showed her appreciation with a smile. 'It's very nice.'

He beamed with pleasure. 'Now, then ... My wife and my friends are shopping at the moment. I've to meet them for lunch back at the hotel. We'll be gone for most of the day and don't expect to be back until late this evening.' He fished a sheet of paper from his inside pocket and handed it to her. 'This is a list of provisions we need. I was going to fetch them myself but this can be your first job.' Next he handed her a card. 'This is the name and address of the supplier. Everything has already been paid for. I'll give you money for a taxi and you can go and collect them some time this afternoon.'

She stopped telling her tale and looked at Fraser resentfully. 'You don't believe a word of this, do you? You think I'm making it up as I go along.'

'Get on with it,' he growled impatiently. 'At the moment I'm keeping an open mind on the matter.'

She glared at him in angry silence for a moment longer then went on, 'Well, there were a lot of provisions. Four medium-sized crates, in fact, and I wondered why they needed so much stuff for a short trip to England. The taxi driver just left me and the crates on the quayside and I had to manhandle them aboard myself.

'Anyway, Mr Smith and his party came back about nine-thirty. He introduced me to his wife and the other couple then he went to the bridge and I heard the engines start up. When we were clear of the harbour

he came down and examined the crates. Three of them
were filled with cans of peaches and he told me to lay
them aside because they were a present for someone
back in England. I thought it odd at the time.
Whoever heard of giving tinned peaches as a present?

'Well, everything went well until last night. I'd been
keeping out of the way as much as possible and just
doing my job. I wasn't keen on the two women,
anyway. In spite of their airs and graces you could
tell they were a pair of hard-bitten good-time girls.
They wore flash jewellery and——'

'Never mind the women,' snapped Fraser. 'I'm only
interested in what happened last night.'

She pouted at him. 'I'm doing my best.' She took
a deep breath then went on...

It had been the sticky patch on the galley floor that
had caught her attention and she had traced the source
to one of the cans of peaches. Rather than let them
go to waste she had pulled the leaking can from the
crate, opened it with a tin-opener and emptied the
contents into a bowl. She had looked at the result and
frowned. A big can and so little an amount of
peaches? She had peered into the empty can and found
that it had been split into two separate compartments.
Turning the can over, she had attacked the bottom
with the opener and spilled the contents on to the
worktop. White powder? My God! It had been co-
caine or something very like it!

'How did you know it was drugs?' Fraser asked
her.

She eyed him scornfully. 'Well, I'm pretty sure it
wasn't talcum powder. Not after the trouble someone
had taken to hide it.'

His mouth twitched and he nodded. 'Go on.'

'Well, I opened another tin and that was the same. And then it suddenly dawned on me that I was the one who'd brought it aboard. If Customs had stopped and searched the boat before we left Portugal Smith could have denied all knowledge of it. He could have said that I applied for the job as cook then used the opportunity to smuggle the drugs myself. It would have been his word against mine. Anyway, that was when Mr Smith came through and caught me. To cut a long story short, he pulled out a gun then locked me in my cabin and said he'd deal with me later.'

'I'd prefer to hear all the details,' Fraser said curtly. 'Everything!'

She shrugged. 'At first he tried to deny that it was drugs, then when he saw that I didn't believe him he tried to bribe me. I told him what I thought of drug dealers and that when we got ashore I was going straight to the police. That's when he got nasty and pulled the gun.'

A shiver ran down her spine. It was probably delayed shock, she told herself. She'd be having nightmares for the next six months and peach melbas would never taste the same. 'He . . . He was going to kill me,' she said in a subdued voice. 'I could see it in his eyes. He only needed to wait until we were further out to sea then he could dump me overboard and watch me drown.'

She closed her eyes and shivered again and suddenly she found herself being supported in Fraser's arms. He held her tightly for a moment and the world stopped swaying.

'I . . . I'm all right now,' she muttered. 'You can let go.'

He led her to a rock and made her sit down then he went to the Land Rover and returned with a flask. 'Take a sip of this. You'll feel better.'

She raised it to her lips and drank, then coughed and spluttered, 'What . . . what was that?'

'Whisky and honey. A well-known remedy around here for everything from depression to pneumonia.'

A warm glow spread throughout her and she breathed deeply at the sweet, clean air. God, it was so good to be alive. Even in a place like this.

As she got to her feet he eyed her closely then, apparently satisfied that she wasn't going to keel over again, he said, 'How did you manage to escape from the locked cabin?'

'I climbed out through the porthole,' she said matter-of-factly. 'It was dark but I knew we were close to the shore. Then I saw the light and I knew there must be people so I jumped.' She shivered again. 'What I didn't bargain for was how cold the water would be. I was frozen stiff and getting cramp. I remember a big wave...and crashing down on a rock... Then waking up in Kirsty's cottage.'

He studied her in silence, his eyes betraying nothing, then he remarked drily, 'That's a pretty far-fetched story.'

She made a sound of disgust. 'I knew you wouldn't believe me.'

'I find it hard to believe that anyone could squeeze themselves through a motor-cruiser porthole. Even someone as slim as you.'

'Well, I did,' she retorted. 'It wasn't easy. I got stuck but managed it in the end.'

'Hmm...' His blue eyes surveyed her again, then he said quietly, 'Take down your jeans.'

Her mouth fell open. 'What ... ?'

'You heard me. Take them down, now.'

She backed away from him in alarm. 'Don't be disgusting. I'll do no such thing.'

His hand reached for her threateningly. 'Perhaps you'd prefer me to do it for you.'

'D-don't you dare lay a finger on me,' she warned. 'I'll scratch your eyes out.'

'For God's sake, girl, be sensible!' he rasped. 'I'm not going to rape you. When I do avail myself of that luscious little body of yours you can rest assured that it'll be in more comfortable surroundings than this.'

His statement that he wasn't going to sexually assault her there and then but that he would definitely get round to it sooner or later did nothing for her peace of mind. 'Then why do you want me to take my jeans off?' she demanded.

'If you had trouble getting through the porthole then you'll have abrasions. Probably on your hips,' he explained slowly. 'I examined you last night for injuries and the only abrasion I saw was on your temple.'

Her cheeks flared at the memory of his hands all over her and she replied heatedly, 'Then you couldn't have looked closely enough. Not that you had any damn right to in the first place.'

His eyes weighed her again, then he growled, 'If there are no marks then I can only assume that everything you've told me is a pack of lies.'

'They're there, I tell you,' she insisted vehemently. 'They were stinging like hell when I had a bath this morning.'

'Then show me.'

'Get lost.'

He took another step towards her and she backed into the Land Rover, her heart thudding at the expression of harsh resolution on his face. 'All right!' she yelled at him. 'Don't touch me. I'll show you.' Turning her back on him, she unzipped her jeans, slid them down over her hips, hooked the hem of her briefs upwards then turned sideways and thrust her hip at him. 'There. See for yourself.'

He grunted. 'Now the other one.'

She repeated the process with her other hip then looked at him resentfully. 'Are you satisfied? Have you seen enough?'

He watched as she hurriedly did up her jeans then his eyes glinted with amusement. 'Yes. For the time being at least. When we get back to the house you can put some ointment on those scratches.'

She looked at him in alarm. 'What house?'

'Mine, of course. You'll be living there from now on.'

The idea didn't appeal to her in the least. It sounded too much like going into the lion's den. 'In your dungeon, no doubt?' she challenged acidly. 'Chained to the wall like the rest of your prisoners? I think I'll decline the invitation if it's all the same to you.'

He gave a sigh of mild irritation. 'I wish you'd stop being so damned awkward. Anyway, you've no option in the matter.'

Now, at last, she had the chance to mock him for a change. 'Of course I have,' she said smugly. 'I can get in touch with the police and give evidence against that gang. No doubt they'll find me accommodation in a hotel until the trial is over, then I can go back to London.'

He shook his head. 'I wouldn't advise it, Avalon. At the moment Smith probably thinks that you drowned last night. If you suddenly turn up as a witness against him then he and his friends might try to implicate you out of sheer spite. It would be a case of your word against theirs, odds of four to one. The judge might not be so easily convinced of your innocence as I was.' He shrugged philosophically. 'It would be a pity seeing someone as young and pretty as yourself languishing in prison for the next ten years.'

Again her spirits plunged and she stared at him bitterly. 'I see. So now it's blackmail, is it? Either I agree to stay here or you'll hand me over to the police?'

'I hadn't thought about that...' he drawled. 'But now that you mention it...'

'You're despicable,' she snorted. 'I think I'd rather spend ten years in prison than be married to a man like you.'

He grinned at her and shook his head. 'No, you wouldn't. Now that I'm satisfied that you aren't a part of that gang after all you'll find me much friendlier.'

Her mouth dropped open as she gaped at him. 'What? Are you seriously telling me that you thought that I...I...?' She spluttered at him in indignation. 'For God's sake! Do I look like a drug smuggler?'

He shrugged. 'I don't know. What do drug smugglers look like? Anyway, you were certainly acting as if you had something to hide when I asked you how you got here.'

'I hate people who deal in drugs,' she muttered, rubbing her hip and thinking of Smith.

'And so do I. At least we've got that much in common.'

She eyed him warily. 'Well, don't let it go to your head. And don't start getting any funny ideas. If I have to stay here I'll feel a lot safer in Kirsty's house than in yours.'

'Out of the question,' he said firmly. 'I can't get to know you better if we're living a mile apart.' He paused and flashed his white teeth at her. 'Besides, Kirsty thinks that it was her fairies that sent you to me. We'd better humour the old dear . . . just in case.'

CHAPTER THREE

As THE Land Rover bounced and rattled its way back along the track Avalon sat tight-lipped, grim-faced and thinking furiously. He was as mad as a hatter, of course. It was the only explanation. And so was Kirsty—which was a shame because she seemed to be such a cheery, harmless old dear. In a way it was also a pity about him because if she'd met him in any other circumstances ... Well, who could tell? You couldn't deny that there was something about him that appealed to the baser instincts, and let's face it, her instincts were just as basic as any other red-blooded woman's. There had been a moment back there when she'd felt light-headed and he'd put his arm around her——

That train of thought came to an abrupt end as he brought the Land Rover to a stop. They'd just passed Kirsty's cottage and were halfway down the hill leading into the village. He pulled on the handbrake then contemplated her with a critical frown. 'Relax,' he growled. 'You look as if you're about to be burnt at the stake.'

She narrowed her green eyes at him. 'You say a thing like that and expect me to relax?'

With a glint of cold humour in the depths of his eyes he began lecturing her. 'News travels fast in a small place like this and everyone will have heard about you by now. They'll be eager to see what kind of woman has been sent to marry their Chief.'

Oh, no! she thought with despair. It couldn't be! Not the whole population? There had to be someone around here whose head was on straight.

'So I'd be obliged if you would at least try to look a little happy at the prospect,' he went on grimly. 'Otherwise they'll feel let down.'

She looked at him rebelliously. 'This is crazy. Surely some of them are bound to wonder how I came to be in the water in the first place?'

'They won't be interested in that,' he declared firmly. 'However, for the benefit of any strangers who turn up, the story will be that you were on holiday, sailing single-handed up the west coast, when you were suddenly caught in a squall and your yacht capsized.' He flashed his teeth at her again in a humourless smile. 'So far I'm the only one who knows about your involvement with the drug smugglers. For your own safety we'll leave it that way.' He paused then added pointedly, 'For the time being at least.'

There was no mistake about that threat—and wasn't that just typical of the kind of man he was? Smile and look happy, or else!

With a final look of warning he released the hand-brake and they drove down the hill into the village. The main street ran past the harbour and halfway along it he pulled up outside a shop which, by means of a weatherbeaten, faded sign above the door, proclaimed itself to be the Suilvach Fashion Emporium. Barely glancing at her, he said brusquely, 'Get out. We've some shopping to do.'

She was quickly learning that when he spoke in that kind of voice it was better just to do as he said. Reluctantly she got out and followed him into the shop.

In spite of its outward appearance the interior of the place came as a surprise. As modern as any large city store, it was well-lit and laid out with racks of skirts, tops, dresses, sweaters.

A bright-eyed little brunette welcomed them with a smile. 'Good morning, Fraser.' She turned to Avalon and said a little breathlessly, 'And you will be the girl from the sea everyone is talking about. You gave old Gavin a terrible fright last night, I can tell you.' At Avalon's look of incomprehension she explained, 'He was the one who found you on the rocks. After he took you to Kirsty's he came straight down to the pub. The poor old soul needed four big drams before he could stop shaking long enough to tell us the story. An hour and six drams later he had to be carried home and put to bed.'

Fraser smiled tolerantly. 'All right, Aileen. Never mind the gossiping. You've got work to do. This young lady's name is Avalon and she has nothing in the world but the clothes she's wearing. I've got business to attend to at the harbour. You've got half an hour to see that she gets everything she needs. If there's anything you haven't got in stock, telephone Oban and have them send it up on the first boat.'

Before Avalon had time to react he'd turned on his heel and marched outside. She blinked, muttered an apology to the girl, then dashed out after him and yelled, 'Wait a minute!'

He stopped, turned and frowned at her. 'What's wrong?'

'What's wrong?' she echoed angrily. 'I'll tell you what's wrong! I don't want any——'

He put his hands on her shoulders and squeezed hard. 'Stop shouting. Aileen is watching from the window. I've already warned you about your behaviour, haven't I?'

She took a deep, steadying breath then demanded in a hoarse whisper, 'Who's going to pay for all this stuff?'

The question seemed to be both irrelevant and unimportant to him and he answered as if to a backward child. 'I am, of course. You're certainly in no position to, are you?'

'I don't want any new clothes,' she hissed. 'I'm quite happy with what I've got. I'll buy a change of clothes as soon as I earn some money.'

'And how are you going to do that?'

'Get a job, of course.' She looked up and down the street. 'There must be someone here who needs a temporary assistant.'

'That's out of the question,' he said harshly. 'And I can't have you walking about like that. You've got a position to maintain. I thought that I'd already made it clear——'

She interrupted him with another fierce whisper. 'I know what your scheme is. You just want to put me in so much debt that I'll have to stay here months to pay it off.'

Her accusation seemed to amuse him. 'Don't be ridiculous. You surely wouldn't deny a man the pleasure of buying a few gifts for his fiancée, would you?'

'I'm not your... your fiancée!' she spluttered.

The smile remained frozen on his face but the tone of his voice became positively menacing. 'We've already discussed this and now you're simply wasting my valuable time. You may not be my fiancée yet but,

until I've decided what to do about you, you'll bloody
well act the part. Is that understood?'

One glance into the cold blue depths of those eyes
was enough and it was all she could do to stop her
teeth from chattering. She nodded her head and replied in a small, meek voice, 'Yes.'

'I've got a name,' he snapped. 'From now on you'll
use it.'

She gave another defeated nod. 'Yes, Fraser.'

'Good. That's better. And from now on when you
address me you'll do so in a respectful manner. No
one yells at a Clan Chief and tells him to "wait a
minute". Is that also understood?'

'Yes . . . Fraser.'

He glanced over her shoulder. 'Now, Aileen is still
watching us and she'll be expecting you to show some
sign of affection and gratitude. We don't want to dis-
appoint her, do we?'

A tiny spark of rebellion flickered briefly in her eyes
then died and she spoke woodenly. 'What kind of
sign?'

'A kiss will do,' he informed her with mock gravity.
'Providing we make it look convincing enough. Just
put your arms around my neck and leave the rest to
me.'

Well, what harm could there be in one little kiss?
she thought weakly. And besides . . . did she have any
choice? There was no place to run to and she had the
uneasy feeling that any further resistance to this man's
demands would snap his patience altogether. He'd
probably throw her back into the sea where she'd come
from.

Hesitantly she raised her arms and by standing on
tiptoe managed to clasp them around his neck. As

close as this to him she was subtly attracted by the clean, well-scrubbed, masculine smell, and she watched in wide-eyed fascination as his hard mouth descended on hers. Her eyelids at last fluttered closed at the warm, tingling sensation on her lips and then, as his strong arms crushed her tighter against him, the tingling became a hot, deep, pulsing throb that vibrated to the very soles of her feet. Other long-dormant physical senses were shaken out of their slumber as she felt her legs driven apart by his hard-muscled thigh and her own soft breasts yielding against his deep, powerful chest.

She made a half-hearted attempt to pull her mouth away but it was only the remains of her dignity making a token gesture for the sake of decency, then all sense of responsibility and all thought of resistance evaporated into a hazy pink fog as his tongue pushed against the barrier of her lips, seeking entry to the riches beyond. She parted her lips and felt the power leave her limbs as she succumbed to his sweet and rapacious plundering.

She began responding . . . Slowly and tentatively at first, then with an ever-increasing avidity as her newly discovered hunger for sensual pleasure demanded more and more. She was nothing but a loose, wanton, thrill-seeking disgrace to womanhood and she didn't give a damn right now. She'd been kissed before but never . . . never had it had an effect like this on her. Every little hormone in her body seemed to be gloriously surfing through her veins in a sea of champagne.

Suddenly it was over and she was left panting as she opened her eyes and saw the look of unexpected pleasure on his face. 'You're pretty good at that,' he murmured lazily. 'We'll need to try it again when we haven't got an audience. Now, get back into the shop before Aileen gets a crick in her neck.'

As he strode off in the direction of the harbour she stood rooted to the spot, still glassy-eyed and trembling. Her excitation by the raw, sexual power of the man on the one hand and her disgust at her lack of self-control on the other hand left her dizzy, in a maelstrom of conflicting emotions. Either he was a demon in disguise or Kirsty had slipped something into her tea at breakfast. Nothing would surprise her from now on.

She took a few deep breaths to give herself time to recover and for the flush to leave her cheeks, then reluctantly she went back into the shop to be welcomed with a glowing smile of approval from Aileen.

'Wait till everyone gets to hear about this!' she exclaimed. 'Now all their worries will be over because everything is going to turn out fine. Didn't I see with my very own eyes how much you love him?' She paused a moment then reflected, 'Mind you, there isn't a woman in Suilvach who wouldn't change places with you if she had the chance.' She sighed dreamily then got down to business. 'Now, then . . . Fraser said you hadn't anything except what you've got on, so we'll start with underwear.' She gave an impish little smile. 'Something nice and sexy, I think?'

'No, thanks,' Avalon said hurriedly. Sexy underwear was the last thing she needed. She was in enough trouble as it was. 'Just plain white cotton will do.'

As she watched the assistant lay out an assortment on the glass-topped counter she had a sudden idea. She hadn't been able to get much sense out of Kirsty in response to her questions and Fraser had coldly

told her to mind her own damned business. But it
now occurred to her that with a little subtle prompting
Aileen might inadvertently provide some of the answers she was seeking. Perhaps she might finally be
able to make a little sense of what was going on around
here.

The problem was knowing where to start without
alerting Aileen to the fact that everything in the garden
wasn't as rosy as she seemed to think. She was examining the underwear and still pondering the
problem when Aileen herself provided the opening by
remarking cheerfully, 'We're all glad for Fraser. When
Kirsty told him that you were coming I don't think
he believed her at first. They say he was awfully surprised when he heard about you turning up here last
night.'

Avalon cleared her throat in embarrassment. 'Yes.
It must have been a bit of a shock, I suppose. I was
pretty surprised myself when I woke up this morning.'

'You'll be needing some skirts and sweaters,' Aileen
said brightly. 'I've got some lovely cashmere...'

Avalon bided her time. There was nothing to be
gained by being impatient and upsetting the girl.

After the skirts and sweaters came trousers and
jeans, and casual outerwear. She made her choices
then remarked in a puzzled voice, 'Kirsty says that
she told Fraser two months ago about me arriving
here. How could she have possibly known that?'

Aileen shrugged and said matter-of-factly, 'Kirsty
is a seer.'

'A seer? What's that?'

'She has visions. She sees things that are going to
happen in the future.'

'Oh, I see. You mean she's a fortune-teller?'

Aileen frowned. 'Aye. In a way, I suppose she is. But not one of those fairground fortune-tellers with a crystal ball and big earrings who just tell you a lot of lies and rubbish. Kirsty has the "gift". Passed down from her great-grandmother, so they say.'

Avalon laughed in spite of herself. 'Well, if she's as good as that she should be down in London making a fortune on the Stock Exchange. She could even ...' Her voice trailed off and she realised that it had been the wrong thing to say when she saw Aileen's lips purse in disapproval.

'If she did that, the "gift" would be taken away from her,' Aileen pointed out solemnly. 'It must only be used for really important things.'

Avalon, acutely aware that she'd blundered into hallowed ground, retreated in embarrassment. 'I...I'm sorry. I wasn't intending to make fun of Kirsty. As a matter of fact she was very good to me. I rather like her.'

Aileen dismissed it. 'Och, it doesn't matter. It must all be strange to you. Our ways are different up here, but you'll soon learn. I went to France last year and I had to spend two days in London. That was all strange to me so I know how you feel.'

Avalon doubted that very much but she kept her mouth shut. She also knew that it was an impossibility for anyone to see into the future, but if the folk up here believed in that sort of thing then good luck to them.

Aileen had begun parcelling up the various items of clothing when suddenly she stopped and came out with an excited torrent of Gaelic—then again she stopped, and looked apologetic. 'Och, I'm sorry. I was forgetting that you're English and don't have the

Gaelic. I was just remembering that you'll be needing something special to wear at the Grand Ceilidh in four weeks' time.'

Four weeks' time! Avalon sincerely hoped that she'd be long gone from here by then. 'What's the Grand Ceilidh?' she asked.

'It's held twice a year,' Aileen said excitedly. 'A big party in the Chief's house. Everyone goes there. Other chiefs and their ladies and the Clan elders and people from America and Australia. You'll have a great time.' She smiled at the prospect, then nodded firmly. 'You'll need a lovely evening dress. I'll order one from Edinburgh.'

Avalon realised that she was just getting sucked deeper and deeper into this mess and she said desperately, 'Look . . . I really don't think you should go to all this trouble.'

'Trouble? What trouble? I've not had such fun for weeks. Anyway, Fraser said I've to order anything you need and you definitely need a dress.' She put her head to one side thoughtfully. 'Now, let's see. It'll have to be the prettiest anyone has ever seen. Especially if Lady Pamela turns up, which she's bound to anyway.'

Avalon heaved a mental sigh. She wasn't even going to ask who the hell Lady Pamela was. This was getting out of hand. With an effort she got back to the job in hand and in a voice of innocent curiosity she probed a little further into the mysteries of this backwater. 'Kirsty mentioned something about a legend. Something about how the wife of the Chief always comes from the sea. I don't understand that. What does it mean?'

Aileen tied the last parcel with a flourish. 'There you are. I can't think of anything else you might be needing. Can you?'

'No. There's more than enough there. Now, I was asking you about this legend?'

Aileen shrugged. 'Aye. It's true enough. They all came from the sea. Just like you.'

'All of them? That's hard to believe.'

Aileen frowned. 'Why? It's true.' She thought for a moment, then went on, 'I don't know about hundreds of years ago, mind you, but I know for a fact that Fraser's mother came from the sea. Fraser's father was in a yacht race and one of the yachts capsized and he pulled this French girl from the sea. They fell in love and got married.' She sighed. 'Isn't that romantic?'

Something cold seemed to brush against the nape of Avalon's neck and she murmured, 'Yes... Very romantic.'

Helpfully Aileen said, 'The best person to ask about these things is Kirsty. She knows all about that kind of stuff.' Her tongue raced on, returning to the subject of the dress she was going to order. 'It'll have to be light green, I think. The same colour as your eyes. Lady Pamela doesn't suit green so you won't clash. She's always beautifully dressed, mind you. She gets all her outfits from Jenners in Edinburgh. Nothing but the best for her.'

A voice growled from the doorway, 'That's enough of the gossip, Aileen.'

Not the least bit put out by the expression of dark displeasure on Fraser's face, the shop assistant grinned at him cheekily. 'We were just discussing the dress Avalon would be wearing to the Grand Ceilidh. I'm sure you want her to be properly dressed for the occasion?'

Avalon clenched her fists in frustration. Dammit! Why couldn't he have stayed away for another five minutes? She'd been patiently working up to the most baffling question of all and hoping that Aileen might know the answer, but it was too late now.

Fraser had relented somewhat and he was regarding Aileen with the kind of patient forbearance of an older brother towards a precociously uninhibited little sister. 'All right. You've done well. Now, please be so kind as to put these parcels in the back of the Land Rover.' When he'd given the order he drew Avalon aside and pressed a wad of banknotes into her hand. 'This is for personal expenses. Let me know when you need more.'

When she saw the amount her eyes widened and she whispered fiercely, 'I don't want your money! You've got me into enough debt as it is.'

He put his mouth closer to her ear and said quietly, 'There's a chemist's shop a few doors down. I suggest you take advantage of it for any items of a personal nature you may require. And get some lipstick while you're at it. Nothing too outrageous, please.'

She flushed with embarrassment then muttered a reluctant thanks and headed for the door. How was it possible to fathom a man like that? she asked herself angrily. One minute he was a cold-eyed tyrant who seemed to delight in humiliating her and imposing his will on her, and then suddenly he could do a thing like this!

When she came out of the chemist the Land Rover was drawn up outside and as she climbed into the passenger seat his blue eyes studied her shrewdly. 'So

Aileen told you about the Grand Ceilidh in a month's time, did she?'

Avalon sat stoically, her hands folded in her lap and her eyes fixed straight ahead. 'Yes. She mentioned something about it.'

He gave a grunt but she ignored it. She was getting used to that sound of disapproval by now. 'Aye...' he said. 'Put two females together and you're bound to get gossip and idle chatter. What else were you discussing?'

'Oh, it was just your usual everyday gossip and idle chatter,' she said sarcastically. 'About fortune-tellers and fairy-tales. That kind of thing.' She scowled and muttered, 'You can tell Aileen not to bother ordering that dress. I won't be here in a month's time.'

'Won't you?' he asked drily. 'I'm sorry to hear that. Isn't our Highland hospitality good enough for you? You'll be used to a much better standard of living than us poor peasants can provide, I suppose?'

His sarcasm, though biting, was justified and she bit her lip in frustration before answering, 'It...it isn't your hospitality. All those new clothes...and the money...and the way Kirsty looked after me. Don't think I'm not grateful for all that.'

He raised an eyebrow. 'What, then?'

She turned in her seat and confronted him angrily. 'First it was Kirsty. And now Aileen. And I suppose everyone else I meet here will be the same. They might be nice and friendly but it's about time they learnt to live in the real world. They talk to me as if I'm not a...a real person with a mind and feelings of my own. As for you—you're even worse because you know the truth about how I got here. But you don't really give a damn about me, do you? Just as long as I keep my mouth shut and act the part . . .'

'Go on,' he urged with deceptive mildness. 'Get it off your chest once and for all.'

'All right! I will,' she snapped. 'You say you intend to keep me here until you've made up your mind whether you want to marry me or not. Do you honestly think that any woman with a scrap of pride would stand for that? This isn't the bloody Middle Ages. Women have got rights nowadays—or hasn't the news reached here yet? I mean . . . even if you did decide to marry me, what are you going to do about it? Drag me kicking and screaming to the altar?'

Their eyes clashed and his lips gave a cynical twist. 'Are you finished?'

She flared her nostrils at him. 'Yes. For the time being.'

The cold smile vanished and his features hardened. 'Right. Now it's my turn. In the first place it's time you learnt a bit of humility. If the people here choose to believe in the folklore that has been handed down through the generations it's their business and no one else's. They don't insist that you share their beliefs but on the other hand they don't appreciate outsiders arriving and ridiculing them.'

She felt a flush of guilt and she protested weakly, 'I don't ridicule them.'

'Yes, you do,' he admonished grimly. 'It's been evident in every word and gesture you've made since you've been with me. It's easy for you to scoff at Kirsty but I have to go along with her. If I ignore her then I lose the respect of my people. They'll feel that I'm betraying them.' His voice softened a little and he shrugged. 'As for dragging you unwillingly to the altar... The people wouldn't stand for that, either. They'd much rather——'

'That's all I hear from you!' she flared. 'The people! The people! Don't upset your precious people! Well, I'm people too, you know. You don't care about upsetting me, do you?'

He ignored her passionate outburst and went on calmly, 'I have to consider the welfare and reputation of my Clan. I would prefer it if the woman I took as my wife was someone they could be proud of. Someone they could look up to. At the moment you don't seem too bright a prospect. When I first saw you last night I had hopes, but my doubts are growing by the minute. By your own admission you threw away your job in a fit of childish pique against your boyfriend. Instead of standing your ground and fighting against the injustice you ran away. Then you stupidly allowed yourself to be duped by a gang of crooks and almost got yourself killed as a result. You're nineteen years old and at the moment you've no job and no money apart from what I've given you. Neither have you any prospects nor any real friends. So far you haven't made much of a success of your life, have you?'

Her face paled at the way he'd stripped away her self-respect with surgical precision and she hissed back at him in a fury, 'I told you right from the start, didn't I? I told you that you were wasting your time with me. I don't belong here. In fact, I'd be the worst possible wife in the world for a man like you. We'd never be away from each other's throats, would we?'

'Aye...' he grunted. 'Once again I suspect that you're right. But there's a problem, and it puts us both in a difficult situation.'

She waited for him to explain, then she burst out, 'I don't see any problem! Just admit that the whole thing is a mistake and put me on the first boat out of here.'

'And how would I explain that to Kirsty and the others?' he asked mockingly. He paused and laughed at the expression of annoyance on her face then said, 'The problem, my bad-tempered little sea-witch, is the mutual sexual attraction we seem to have for each other. The more I think of that, the more I find myself weighing it in your favour.'

A smile of cold contempt and a disdainful toss of the head might have done the trick and put him in his place. Either that or a torrent of heated invective. Instead, she found herself absolutely tonguetied for a full ten seconds, then she stammered, 'Th—that's ridiculous! I don't feel the least bit like that about you.'

He drew back and looked at her in feigned astonishment. 'You don't? Well, now, that really surprises me, Avalon. When I kissed you earlier on you seemed to become quite agitated. Abandoned, even. It's a good job I stopped when I did or who knows what kind of a public exhibition you might have made of yourself?'

She was too embarrassed to say anything, and, although she turned away to stare grimly through the windscreen, she was acutely aware of his blue eyes studying her reaction with amusement.

'Ah, well . . .' he said at last. 'If you insist that you felt nothing then I must have been mistaken. I'll just have to try harder next time.'

'There won't be a next time,' she muttered angrily. 'I'll make damned sure of that.'

'Hmmm...' He nodded to himself thoughtfully. 'Ah, yes... I was forgetting. You've reached the ripe old age of nineteen and you tell me that you're still a virgin. Now that would indicate a degree of tenacious resolution and strict self-denial that one can only applaud.' He patted her thigh, sending tiny involuntary tremors through her entire body. 'Good. Excellent. There's nothing I like better than a challenge. Especially when the prize is so desirable.'

'The last man who tried to take me by force still has a limp and the marks of my nails on his face,' she warned him coldly.

'Tut-tut,' he chided in soft mockery. 'Who said anything about force?'

'Well, if you intend relying on nothing but your charm and personality you aren't going to get very far with me,' she retorted.

'No?' He gave a short laugh. 'We'll see. Perhaps the party tonight will inflame those little red corpuscles in your blood and put you in the mood.'

'Party?' She looked at him in astonishment, then made a noise of derision. 'I'm not going to any party. You can forget that for a start. I can't think of one single thing I feel like celebrating.'

He pinched the bridge of his nose between finger and thumb and sighed. 'You're going to the party whether you want to or not. The whole village will be there and they'll be expecting to see you by my side, smiling and enjoying yourself.' He paused and looked at her in exasperation. 'I don't like having to repeat myself but I'll say this one last time and you'd better take heed. From now on you'll do exactly what you're told, without excuses or arguments. Is that finally getting through to you, Miss Rivers?'

Her eyes smouldered with resentment as she remembered the hold he had over her and she spoke through clenched teeth. 'Yes.'

'Yes, what?' he growled.

She swallowed and muttered, 'Yes, Fraser.'

'Good.' He studied her a moment longer, then he squeezed her thigh once more and smiled with anticipation. 'Now that that's all settled we can go home and relax.'

Relax? Oh, that was funny! That was hysterically funny! She closed her eyes and chewed worriedly at her lip. Relax? Ye gods!

CHAPTER FOUR

FRASER dumped the parcels at the foot of the bed—a double bed, she noted with alarm, the duvet thrown back to reveal crisp, white linen sheets. 'I had the housekeeper prepare this room this morning.' His blue eyes contemplated her as she took in the rest of her surroundings then he said drily, 'Not quite the dungeon you were expecting, is it?'

He strolled across the room and threw a door open. 'This is the bathroom. If there's anything you need, tell Mrs MacKay. She'll see to it.'

Try as she might there was nothing about the room she could justifiably find fault with. Large and airy, it was decorated in a muted, pastel shade of pink. There were fresh flowers in a vase on the dressing-table and the pile on the light grey carpet felt thick and luxurious beneath her feet. The window over-looked the trees outside and provided a panoramic view across the blue waters of the bay towards the village.

'If you don't like it you're welcome to share the master bedroom with me,' he offered amiably. 'It's much larger than this. Perhaps you'd like to see it now so that you can make up your mind?'

Sniffing with disdain, she marched back to the heavy oak door and made great play about examining the lock. 'Is there a key for this thing?'

'On the dressing-table.'

'Good. In that case this room will do fine.'

'Well, in that case I'll leave you to get settled in,' he responded with dry politeness. He gestured at the parcels. 'I suggest you look out something cool to wear at the party tonight. Social gatherings here tend to quicken the heart and stir the blood.'

As soon as he'd gone she grabbed the key, turned it in the lock and heard the reassuring clunk as it shot home. If the notion came over him she had no doubt that he was capable of kicking the door off its hinges, but even an illusion of security was better than nothing, she told herself.

Her first sight of the house, from Kirsty's cottage, hadn't really prepared her for the real thing. It had been half hidden behind a stand of pine trees and what she had managed to make out had looked imposing enough but, when the Land Rover had drawn up at the front door, the sheer size and grandeur of the place had taken her breath away and it had been an effort to maintain her air of bored indifference.

Three storeys high and built of durable granite blocks, it blended perfectly into the background of crags and heather-covered slopes. Square towers at either end and battlements across the roof proved that whichever of Fraser's ancestors had built this place hadn't been short of enemies.

With a feeling of dismay and a considerable lack of enthusiasm she'd followed him up the broad steps and through the arched doorway.

In the hallway he'd dumped her parcels on a table and ordered her brusquely to stay where she was while he went in search of his housekeeper. She'd taken the opportunity to look around the vast hall. The walls were panelled in wood just a shade darker than the gleaming parquet flooring. Doors led to various other rooms and on her left a broad staircase led to the upper reaches of the house. There was a rich smell of old leather and polish in the air. At the far end of the hall a corridor led to what was probably the kitchen, and if you closed your eyes you could almost imagine the scantily clad serving-wenches running to and from the banqueting-hall with trays of food and flagons of wine for their lord and master.

At the mention of a housekeeper she'd drawn a crumb of comfort from the knowledge that there would be someone else in the house apart from their two selves, but he'd returned a few minutes later muttering something about never being able to find 'that woman' when you needed her. She'd cast him a look of doubt and suspicion then decided that he was probably telling the truth. Someone around here had to do the cleaning and she couldn't imagine him prancing about with a Hoover and feather duster.

With an expression of mild irritation he'd gathered up her parcels then grunted, 'Your room is upstairs. Follow me.'

Now, with a bit of privacy at last, she perched herself on the edge of the bed and took stock of her situation. Well, she had comfortable accommodation, a brand new wardrobe of clothes and more spending money than she usually got through in a month. She was even being taken to a party tonight! For a girl who'd been stranded and penniless a few days ago she didn't have any right to complain. Except for that impossible man, of course. Fraser of Suilvach. Old Blue Eyes himself.

How could any woman hope to deal with a man like him?

About the only thing to be said for him was that he was honest. Or, to be more precise, he didn't believe in being devious or beating around the bush. He'd made it brutally clear that, although he had no particular liking for her as a person, he intended to bundle her into bed as soon as he got half a chance, merely to satisfy his lust. He might be the Lord of the Deer and Eagles but he had all the moral conscience of a hungry tiger.

As far as she could see her only hope was to keep one step ahead of him, but she doubted if she had the stamina or he had the patience.

Sighing, she got to her feet and began unwrapping the parcels. Selecting a pair of dark blue cord trousers and a white polo-necked sweater, she changed out of her own clothes and studied the effect in the mirror. Next she brushed the tangles from her long hair and applied the merest touch of coral-pink lipstick then gave her reflection another critical once-over. Thankfully the sweater wasn't too tight. The man was hot-blooded enough without her doing anything to raise his temperature. Finally, after dragging it out for as long as she could, the remainder of the clothes were hung away carefully in the wardrobe and she ventured nervously downstairs.

At the foot of the stairs she stopped and listened for any sound of life but the house remained silent. Across the hall from her one door was slightly ajar and she approached it with caution. There was no reply to her knock and, holding her breath, she pushed the door wider and entered.

Her gaze travelled over the artistic panelling of the walls, the shelves of books, the massive leather-topped desk and the deep chesterfield armchairs. There was an atmosphere of quiet privacy about the room that heightened her feeling of intrusion and she was about to retreat when she saw the row of silver-framed photographs above the blackened stone fireplace and her curiosity impelled her to have a closer look.

With one quick, nervous glance over her shoulder she tiptoed across the room and reached up to the mantelpiece.

The first photograph showed a middle-aged couple smiling up into the camera from the seat of an open sports car. The woman was a stunning, dark-eyed beauty and if these were Fraser's parents it was obvious where he'd got his looks. The next photograph showed the same couple in formal evening wear at some society function.

The next three pictures were of Fraser. The first showed him as a boy about ten, proudly holding a fish he'd just caught. The second showed him in a kilt, being awarded a prize at some sporting event. The last photograph was a studio portrait of him in cap and gown holding a rolled-up diploma.

She'd just replaced it on the mantelpiece when she almost jumped out of her skin as a pair of hands came from behind and cupped her breasts. Rigid with shock, she felt warm breath on her neck and heard him say, 'A perfect fit. Almost made to measure for me, wouldn't you say?'

Firmly she removed his hands, then turned and confronted him angrily. 'That wasn't a very nice thing to do.'

His mouth quirked in a sardonic smile. 'On the contrary, Avalon. It was very nice. It gave me considerable pleasure. Your body excites me. I find the need to touch it quite irresistible.'

'I was talking about the way you sneaked up on me,' she said crossly.

His blue eyes taunted her. 'Do you mean that you don't mind me touching you so long as I give you adequate warning?'

She gave an explosive sigh. It didn't matter what you said to this man, he would twist your words and meaning. 'I'd rather you didn't touch me at all,' she snapped heatedly. 'And I'll feel a damn sight safer when your housekeeper is around. Have you found her yet?'

'No. But she can't be far.' He glanced around the room. 'I thought that she might have been the one who let you in here.'

'The door was open.' She eyed him sullenly. 'I wasn't prying, if that's what you're thinking.'

He made an all-encompassing sweep of his arm. 'Pry to your heart's content. I'll give you a guided tour of the house if you like. The sooner you feel at home, the better.'

'Better for whom?' she asked tartly. 'I'll never feel at home here. The place is too damned big for a start. I feel lost.'

'You'll get used to it,' he assured her easily. 'Anyway, you can't expect a Clan Chief to live in a fisherman's cottage, can you?' He looked around the room in pleasure. 'I'm quite fond of the ancestral pile.' He gestured at the shelves. 'There are hundreds of books so you needn't worry about getting bored. There's a stereo with plenty of tapes and discs if you prefer listening to music.' He paused and grinned at her. 'Of course I'll always be on hand if you should feel the need for something more energetic in the way of recreation.'

'Yes . . .' she muttered. 'That's just what I'm afraid of.' She pointed to the picture of him holding the diploma. 'What did you study at university? The art of abduction and seduction?'

The smile remained on his face. 'No. That's a degree in construction and civil engineering.'

She sniffed. 'Then why aren't you doing something useful like building roads in Africa instead of playing at lord of the manor up here?'

'Actually, it was India,' he said quietly. 'And it wasn't roads. I was building hospitals.' He reached past her and picked up a picture of the middle-aged couple. 'I had to return here when my parents were killed in an accident.' He gazed at the picture a moment longer, his eyes clouded with memories, then he replaced it and said coldly, 'As for playing "lord of the manor", you're also wrong about that. The livelihoods of over two thousand families here depend on my business skills and dedication to the moral obligation placed upon me.'

She lowered her eyes and mumbled an apology. 'I . . . I'm sorry. I didn't mean to . . .'

He turned and marched towards the door and she winced at the apparently cold rejection of her apology, then to her surprise she saw that he was waiting on her to join him. As if the incident had never happened he said briskly, 'Come on. I'll show you the main feature of the house.'

Taking her by the arm, he led her across the hallway. Throwing open a door, he flicked on a switch.

She drew a deep breath of stunned admiration. From the ceiling hung a glittering chandelier which cast slivers of brilliant light on to the polished oak floor. At the far end of the huge room a fireplace

large enough to roast an ox was flanked by suits of
armour. The walls were hung with ancient banners,
coats of arms, shields and ancestral portraits. He
began talking about the Grand Ceilidh which was tra-
ditionally held in this room, but she was too over-
awed to take in his words and she gawped at her
surroundings like a dumbstruck tourist in a stately
home.

Her trance was broken as a voice spoke from the
doorway. 'Fraser, have you been looking for me?'

'Ah, Mrs MacKay! Come in. This is Avalon.'

The housekeeper was a slim, well-preserved sixty-
year-old with a friendly smile and a warm, reassuring
handshake that helped to lift Avalon's spirits a little.
'I'm sorry I was out when you arrived,' she apologised. 'I was helping the gamekeeper's wife with her
twins. They've got the measles.'

'It's all right,' Fraser assured her. 'I've shown
Avalon her room.'

'Aye. But I don't suppose you thought to offer the
poor lassie a cup of tea, did you?' She reached for
Avalon's arm. 'You come with me through to the
kitchen and we'll have a wee blether.'

Avalon hesitated for a moment and glanced en-
quiringly at Fraser, but he merely shrugged off his
housekeeper's criticism goodnaturedly and said, 'I'll
see you later. I've got plenty of other business to
attend to.'

The kitchen was bright and modern and the tea
sweet and hot. Mrs MacKay beamed at her across the
table. 'Well, Kirsty was right when she told me over
the phone. You are very beautiful.'

She looked away in embarrassment. 'That's not the
word I'd use, Mrs MacKay.'

'All right. Let's just say, very attractive and modest. Is your room comfortable enough for you, Avalon?'

'Yes. It...it's very nice.' She gazed around the kitchen. 'The whole house is...' She paused awkwardly, wondering what to say without appearing too silly. 'It...it's huge. I don't know how you manage on your own.'

There was a drawn-out silence and she could feel herself being studied shrewdly from behind that friendly smile, then Mrs MacKay said quietly, 'You're frightened of this place, aren't you, Avalon? I could see it on your face when you were in the ballroom.'

Frightened? Had it been that obvious? She gave an embarrassed smile. 'I think I found it a bit...well, unexpected. A bit grander than anything I've ever been used to.'

The housekeeper nodded wisely. 'Aye. That's exactly how Giselle felt when the old Chief brought her here.'

'Giselle?'

'Fraser's mother. She was French.'

Avalon remembered the dark-eyed beauty in the photograph. She also remembered the story Aileen had told her and she asked innocently, 'Is it true that they met when her yacht capsized?'

Mrs MacKay eyed her shrewdly again. 'You've heard about the legend, haven't you?'

Avalon toyed with her cup, weighing her answer carefully. Fraser's warning about ridiculing the beliefs of the locals was still fresh in her mind, as was his strict injunction to act the part of his loving fiancée whether she felt it or not. Anything out of place said to Mrs MacKay had a good chance of reaching his ears and bringing more of his wrath down upon her.

'Well...' she began hesitantly. 'I suppose there must be something behind it.'

Mrs MacKay laughed. 'Aye, well it's true enough about his mother. During the annual Western Isles yacht race, it was. Thirty-odd years ago. And twenty years before that the captain of a Navy frigate picked up the survivors of the *Athenia*. That was a liner that was torpedoed at the beginning of the war. There was a young American girl called Martha...'

Again Avalon felt that tiny shiver run down her spine and her eyes widened. 'Fraser's grandparents?'

Mrs MacKay nodded, then smiled benignly. 'And now there's you. Shipwrecked and washed ashore. Come from the sea just like the rest of them. Call it a legend...or coincidence...or history repeating itself. It makes you think, doesn't it?' She poured another two cups of tea and went on quietly, 'What I'm really trying to tell you, Avalon, is that when Giselle first arrived she was as confused as you are. It may be a romantic way to find a husband but to suddenly find yourself about to be saddled with all the duties and responsibilities of the First Lady of the Clan... To be surrounded by all the history and tradition that goes along with this place...' She sighed. 'I can understand how you feel.'

Avalon doubted that very much, but there was no way she could reveal the true situation to Mrs MacKay.

When they'd finished their tea the housekeeper got to her feet and said briskly, 'Well, there's plenty of time before I start preparing the evening meal. Why don't you come with me and I'll show you over the rest of the house and the grounds? After all, since you're going to spend the rest of your life here, I'm sure you can't wait to see everything for yourself.'

Pinning a smile of bright eagerness to her face, but inwardly groaning at her own deceit, she nodded. 'Yes. I'd like that.'

She'd dressed herself in a light blue cotton blouse and short, pleated skirt and it was eight-thirty in the evening when she presented herself for Fraser's inspection in the library downstairs. He stood by the fire, a glass of whisky in his hand, and ran his eye over her critically.

Flushing under his scrutiny, she said, 'You told me I was to wear something cool and light.'

'Aye. So I did.' His gaze travelled the length of her body slowly, then he nodded in satisfaction. 'Very fetching.'

He, too, was dressed almost too casually in faded, worn chinos and a white, open-necked shirt, but she had to admit grudgingly that he was the kind of man who'd look lethally attractive no matter what he chose to wear.

She was anything but thrilled at the prospect of meeting a crowd of his friends and she remarked bitterly, 'I'm not looking forward to this party, you know. Everyone will be staring at me and you'll be expecting me to walk around all evening with a stupid smile on my face pretending that I'm enjoying myself.'

'You'll have a good time,' he said drily. 'Just take my word for it. Anyway, you've no choice in the matter. Donny McLeod has specially asked to meet you. It's his greatest wish.'

'Well, I've no wish to meet him,' she replied tartly. 'Nor any other of your cronies, come to that.'

She saw his eyes grow bleak then he said quietly, 'Donny is one hundred and two years old today and the party is in his honour. Like everyone else he's heard about your arrival and he wants to meet the *caileagh bhan* from the sea before it's too late.'

'Oh...' She bit her lip then eyed him resentfully. 'If you had told me that at the start...' She paused and frowned. 'What's a *caileagh bhan*?'

'Fair-haired girl.' He drained his glass, set it down on the mantelpiece, then handed her a small, gift-wrapped box. 'This is a present from us to him. I want you to hand it over. It'll please the old man.'

'Yes. Of course.' She weighed the box in her hand. 'Shouldn't I know what it is?'

'A new briar pipe and a pound of his favourite tobacco.'

She looked at him in disbelief. 'He's a hundred and two and he still smokes?'

He shrugged. 'Aye. And he still manages to get through half a bottle of whisky a day. And he's still got an eye for the ladies, so don't be surprised if he makes a pass at you.'

She caught the gleam of ironic amusement in his eyes and she pursed her lips in annoyance and snapped, 'Come on, then. Let's get it over with before I change my mind.'

The sun had dipped below the western sea and the first stars were appearing in the sky when they drew up outside the village hall. Across the road the harbour was crowded with boats, their masthead lights swaying and bobbing. The front door of the hall was open, allowing light and the noise of laughter to spill outside, and her misgivings returned. Every eye was going to be on her the moment she stepped through that door. She was bound to do or say something stupid.

Her nervousness was only increased when Fraser gripped her by the shoulders and looked grimly down into her face. 'A word of warning before we go in. I want this party to be a success for Donny's sake. Don't let me down. Just remember who you're supposed to be and try to act accordingly.'

She glared up at him for a moment in angry silence, then sighed and looked away. 'I'll try my best but I'm not giving any guarantees. I never was much good at acting.'

'Well, you'd better try for an Oscar tonight,' he said ominously. He entwined his fingers in her hair, forced her head back, then bared his teeth like a wolf contemplating a chicken. 'Perhaps you need a kiss to instil a little motivation for the part.'

Her green eyes widened in alarm and she stammered, 'Th-that won't be necessary. I...I don't need——' Her words came to a strangled end as he crushed his mouth against hers. The ferocity of the unprovoked assault on the tenderness of her lips went on and on, aided and abetted by the insidious probing of his tongue. At last the bruising contact softened, inviting her to break loose, but her legs were powerless, her heart was hammering and her own lips were tingling and heated with too much excitement to pay much attention to anything else. He released her, leaving her gasping and half dazed. 'Well?' he growled. 'Has that put you in the mood or do you want more?'

She gulped. What kind of stupid question was that to ask a woman? she wondered vaguely.

He gave a slightly wicked grin and cupped her face in his hands. 'Left you speechless, I see. And dewy-eyed with desire. That's a good sign. Now, just hang

on to my arm as if you really meant it and we'll go
in.'

There was a crowd standing just inside the doorway
and they smiled in welcome and parted respectfully
as Fraser made his entrance. By his side, and trying
desperately to look calm and collected, she glanced
around the hall, noting the tables loaded with food
and drink, the bunting hanging from the walls and
ceiling, the four-piece band on the stage at the far
end, the older folk sitting and relaxing with their
drinks while the younger ones milled around ex-
changing banter. There was no mistaking the guest of
honour as he sat, flanked by his equally ancient rela-
tives, at a large table in front of the low platform. As
Fraser led her across the room the conversation
dropped to a murmur, then died away. Stopping in
front of the old man, Fraser grinned. 'The *caileagh
bhan* has come to pay her respects and wish you a
happy birthday, Donny.'

The old man looked up, his eyes bright and lively
in an incredibly wrinkled, weatherbeaten face.
Studying her, he finally nodded to himself in satisfaction and smiled.

'We...we brought you a birthday present, Mr
McLeod.' Trying not to look too awkward and embarrassed, she laid the gift in front of him. His hand
reached out and caught hers and she blinked in surprise as he raised it to his lips and kissed it lightly.

There was a row of full whisky glasses on the table.
Fraser lifted one, then raised it in salutation and began
talking in Gaelic. Having made the toast, he swallowed
the drink in one gulp, as seemed to be the custom,
then he picked up another glass and thrust it into her
hand. Painfully aware of the silence and the watchful

eyes, she racked her brains for something suitable to say, then she, too, raised her glass and smiled. 'I came here to honour you, Mr McLeod, but I was the one who was honoured when you kissed my hand. I drink to the continued good health of a truly gallant old gentleman.' The whisky burned her throat but, determined not to give herself a showing up, she gulped it down to a loud murmur of approval.

'My God!' she spluttered to Fraser when they'd moved out of earshot. 'My stomach is on fire. I'm going to be sick.'

He gripped her arm tightly. 'Don't you dare. The feeling will pass in a moment or two but you'd better stick to lemonade for the next couple of hours.' Her stomach gave a few more involuntary shudders then calmed down. It seemed to be the signal for the band, and as they struck up a waltz Fraser took her in his arms. They did one complete circuit of the floor while everyone looked on, then other couples paired off and joined in.

'You're quite a good dancer,' he murmured in her ear. 'As nimble with your feet as you are with your tongue. That was an impressive toast you made to Donny. You're a better actress than you give yourself credit for.'

'That was no act,' she retorted. 'He's an impressive old man. I meant every word I said.'

The waltz finished and there was an immediate roll of drums and an announcement from the stage in Gaelic. Fraser shrugged and led her to a table. 'You'd better sit this one out. It's an eightsome reel.'

The chance to defy him and assert her independence was too good to miss. Besides, the fire in her stomach had settled to a pleasant glow and she felt reckless. 'I'm not sitting down yet,' she argued. 'You said that I'd enjoy myself and that's what I intend doing. You can teach me the dance as we go along.'

He eyed her doubtfully. 'It's a fast and complicated dance.'

'So?'

He saw the adamant tilt to her chin and shrugged as if to say, OK, you asked for it. He took her arm and led her back on to the floor where other couples were already forming up in squares. An instant's doubt assailed her when the wildly intoxicating beat of the music started up, but her hands were grabbed on either side of her and she was swept willy-nilly into the exciting rhythm and gyrations of the reel.

It was only by her quick wits and reflexes that she managed to complete the dance without falling on her backside and making a fool of herself, and as Fraser led her off the floor she gasped, 'Now I know why you told me to wear something cool.'

'Aye...' he drawled, looking her up and down. 'You need to exercise. You're out of breath and out of condition.'

Trust him to find something to moan about, she thought. She narrowed her eyes at him but before she could think of a suitable answer to his criticism he changed the subject. 'We can't keep dancing with each other. You and I will be expected to mingle with the other guests. There are a few old ladies here who'll be grievously offended if their Chief doesn't ask them up to dance. Rank imposes its obligations.'

'I know all about *noblesse oblige*,' she sniffed. 'And you needn't worry about me. I'll just have another drink and——'

'Do what you like, but go easy on the whisky,' he warned. 'Don't get drunk. I've got plans for you when we get home.'

He gave her a quick kiss on the cheek, then turned his back on her and made his way down the hall.

She stared after him uneasily. Plans? That sounded vaguely threatening—especially if he meant what she thought he meant. Well, they'd see about that. There was an old saying, wasn't there? Something about the best-laid plans of mice and men...and blue-eyed Clan Chiefs who seemed to think they were irresistible.

Sighing, she turned to the table and helped herself to a can of Coke. The people around her were laughing and chatting away to one another and she wished she understood the strange-sounding language. The fact that she didn't only seemed to emphasise the point that she didn't really belong here and never would. Occasionally she caught a few shy glances and tentative smiles coming her way, and she responded likewise, but that seemed to be as far as her contact with the locals would ever get.

'Hello, Avalon. Enjoying the party?'

The sound of the familiar voice raised her spirits and she turned and smiled in relief at Aileen. 'I'm just recovering my breath after that dance.'

The shop-girl laughed. 'Aye. I saw you and Fraser on the floor. If you think the eightsome reel is fast just wait till they play "Strip The Willow". It's lethal. Take my advice and sit it out.' She paused and looked around. 'Where is Fraser, by the way?'

'Being sociable. Spreading his charm around.' She hoped she hadn't sounded too caustic and she added quickly, 'I'm supposed to do the same but it's hard when you don't know anyone.'

'Aye. That's just like a man, isn't it? Anyway, you know me. We'll have a drink then I'll take you round and break the ice.' She paused, then said wryly, 'Lady Pamela would never have allowed Fraser to leave her on her own at a party like this. She'd have been sticking to him like a leech.' She opened a can of fruit juice then added, 'I don't know what he sees in her. She's a stunner to look at but Fraser isn't stupid. He must know what she's really like.'

Avalon hated gossip and it was only politeness and a reluctance to appear uninterested in Aileen's opinions that prompted her to say, 'Surely she can't be that bad?'

'No? Wait till you meet her. She isn't a real lady, of course. That's just what we call her behind her back.' Suddenly she groaned, bit her lip, then said desperately, 'Look . . . You . . . you won't tell Fraser, will you? He might not like it.'

Avalon reassured her with a sympathetic smile. 'Of course I won't.'

Aileen still looked uncomfortable and she muttered, 'Fraser is right. I do talk too much. I should learn to keep my mouth shut.' She sipped her drink reflectively then cheered up. 'It doesn't matter, anyway. When you and Fraser are married she'll have no reason to come here again.'

It was time to change the subject, Avalon told herself firmly. Adopting another smile, she said, 'How about those friends of yours? Are you going to introduce me . . . ?'

It was just before midnight, with still no sign of the party breaking up, when Fraser told her that it was time to leave. Pleasantly exhausted and light-headed, she followed him out and slumped into the passenger seat of the Land Rover.

'I'm glad to see that you took my advice about staying reasonably sober,' he commented as he started the engine.

For the first time since she'd met him he actually sounded pleased with her. Well, wonders would never cease, would they? she thought. 'It wasn't easy,' she replied. 'Up here everyone seems to feel naked unless they've got a glass in their hand.' She laughed. 'Now I know why the Scots invented whisky. It's to give them the energy for all that wild dancing.'

'Aye...' He chuckled, his eyes fixed on the road ahead. 'You may be right.'

In the darkness all she could make out was the strong, craggy profile of his face, and she wondered if she was actually beginning to like him. Falling in love with him was out of the question, of course. Just because she had this insane desire to reach out and touch him... to feel his lips on hers once more... That wasn't love. It couldn't be. It was only the excitement of the evening and the fire in her veins.

While talking to Aileen and the other girls at the party she'd been able to read between the lines and get a deeper insight into Fraser and the people in this part of the country.

Honest... dependable... fair-minded. Name any good quality you were looking for in a man and Fraser had it in abundance. It was true that he kept it hidden most of the time under a shell of granite, but it was there. There wasn't a woman in Suilvach who wasn't in love with him and yet none of them seemed to resent the fact that she, an outsider, had suddenly appeared, ostensibly to claim him as her own. It was the old legend come true again and none of them was prepared to argue with that. They might envy her, but if Fate had chosen her to be the lucky one then she must surely deserve the honour and happiness. That had shaken her. Such altruism was beyond her experience. It was the complete opposite of her previous knowledge of a world which seemed to be filled with nothing but back-stabbing opportunists and self-serving wretches.

She was still pondering the question when they reached the house. He led her inside, closed the front door behind them, then took her by the arm and guided her into the library. The remains of a log fire cast a warm red glow in the darkness and the pulse in her neck quickened in a delicious mixture of fear and anticipation. 'I . . . I really think I should go to bed, Fraser. We . . . we can talk tomorrow.'

He switched on a tiny desk lamp and she saw the determined gleam in his blue eyes. 'No, Avalon. We'll talk now. I think it's time we got to know more about each other.'

CHAPTER FIVE

AVALON stood by the fireplace and accepted the drink he'd poured—a small measure of malt whisky mixed with plenty of water. Taking a quick sip, she placed the glass on the mantelpiece and eyed him nervously. 'All right. What is it you want to talk about?'

He raised a mocking eyebrow. 'You and me. What else?' He sipped his own drink, those disturbing blue eyes regarding her with amusement over the rim. 'Did you enjoy the party?'

'Yes.' She felt tense and uneasy and wished her legs would stop trembling. 'As a matter of fact, I did. I had a marvellous time.'

'Good.' He nodded in apparent satisfaction. 'I was glad to see you entering into the spirit of the occasion.' He laid his own glass down and advanced towards her. 'Now we'll see how well you enter into the spirit of this occasion.'

If she'd had any doubts about his intentions they were swept away as his fingers began to unbutton her blouse. Instinctively her hands came up to push him away, then they dropped to her sides as she surrendered to the inevitability of what was going to happen to her. She might conceivably find the strength to thwart him, but she couldn't fight the burning, aching desire of her own body. Even the mere brushing of his fingers against the sensitive skin of her neck was sending tremors of excitement through every nerve.

As he reached the third button his eyes bored into hers and he said quietly, 'I don't intend marrying a woman who is incapable of enjoying a healthy sexual relationship.'

'And you intend to try before you buy?' She'd meant to sound mocking and sarcastic but the husky tremor in her voice robbed it of any conviction.

He was down to the last button now, and the deep shadows on his face shifted as he grinned and said, 'Yes. And to match your cliché—better safe than sorry.' When her blouse was open he slid it gently over her shoulders and down her arms until it fluttered to rest on the sheepskin rug at her feet. Pulling her unresisting body closer, he deftly undid the clasp of her bra and, when it too had fallen to the floor, he held her at arm's length and feasted his eyes on her nakedness.

At any other time she'd have been mortified with embarrassment but the obvious pleasure on his face thrilled and filled her with a heady exhilaration and she could feel her nipples hardening under the mere caress of those eyes.

Pulling her towards him once more, he set her mouth alight with a blistering kiss and she was only dimly aware of the zipper of her skirt giving way. Keeping on with the relentless assault on her swollen and tender lips, he completed her undressing then he released her and stepped backwards. In the firelight her skin glowed golden, and once more she shamelessly revelled in his look of awed admiration.

'My God...' he whispered reverently. 'You're beautiful, Avalon. So lusciously desirable.'

Dry-mouthed with mounting excitement, she watched through half-closed lids as he quickly undressed himself, and then it was her turn to gasp in fascination. The soft glow that bathed her own body gave him the appearance of some virile Greek god sculpted in bronze and copper.

Proud and erect, he swept her masterfully into his arms and as their mouths again made sweet contact she felt his hand moving with tactile sensitivity down over the contour of her breast to pause and stroke her nipple then continue lower, over the flatness of her stomach, and down towards... The power drained from her legs as his fingers slid between her thighs and she wrenched her mouth away from his and bit into his shoulder with a stifled gasp. Slowly they both sank to the floor and she stared up at him through eyes unable to focus as his hand stimulated her to an erotic frenzy.

He stilled the fluttering pulse in her neck with a kiss, then his lips burned a slow, glazing trail over her soft, yielding flesh towards the hard, aching tautness of her swollen nipple.

A low, deep moaning sound escaped her lips and her fingers scrabbled wildly in his hair as he shifted his weight on top of her. She felt her legs being driven apart and her body arced upwards in response to his urgent demand. There was a brief, sharp pain as he thrust himself deeply into the sweet dark warmth, and another moan of sensual delirium rose from her throat as he began a slow rhythmic movement inside her.

Oblivious of everything but the incandescent fire that seemed to be melting every nerve in her body, she buried her face in his neck and rode the waves of raging passion. The taste and smell of him was in her mouth and nostrils, inflaming and goading her towards undreamed-of heights. She heard a low, almost animal-sounding growl resonate in his throat, then as he released the pent-up flood of his own passion her body convulsed uncontrollably and she dug her fingers deep into the hard muscles of his back.

The raging storm subsided, the floodtide ebbed, and he kissed her eyelids gently until her laboured breathing returned to normal. He eased his weight from her and turned her so that they lay facing each other. His brow was damp and glistening, she noticed, and she smiled at him with a slow, lazy contentment. 'I told you I was a virgin, didn't I?'

He kissed the tip of her nose and toyed with the lobe of her ear. 'I never doubted it for one minute.'

'Liar,' she murmured. 'And you just couldn't wait to find out the truth for yourself, could you?'

His blue eyes taunted her. 'Just as you couldn't wait to prove it. And, judging by the noises you were making, you thoroughly enjoyed the experience.'

She smiled at him lazily again. 'What chance does an innocent little girl have against a man like you? A couple of drinks...a luxurious rug in front of a log fire...the lights down low. How many women have you lured into this little lovenest? I wonder.'

His fingers were gently massaging the back of her neck. 'I've lost count. Does it worry you?'

She bent her head, kissed him on the nipple play-fully, then murmured, 'No. But I was wondering how I compared with the rest of them.'

He pretended to consider for a moment, then grinned. 'Pretty near the top.'

'Only pretty near?' she teased. 'Hmmm...You've hurt my feelings. If you were a real gentleman you'd have lied and said I was the best.'

He shrugged. 'All right. You were the best. The others were nothing compared to you.'

'Even better than Pamela?' she asked innocently.

He stiffened and sat up as if she'd stabbed a finger at a raw nerve, and she flinched at the sudden change of mood from loving warmth to obvious irritation. 'The relationship between me and Pamela has nothing to do with you,' he snapped.

The hurt in her eyes quickly changed to hot resentment and, after they'd both hurriedly dressed, she challenged him fiercely. 'She's your girlfriend, isn't she?'

His face darkened. 'I told you that it's none of your business.'

She glared at him in shocked disbelief. Were all men as brutally insensitive as him? she asked herself. He'd lifted her to the heights and now he was dumping her firmly back in her place. 'Of course it's my business,' she fumed. 'I was a virgin until a few minutes ago. I let you make love to me. Doesn't that entitle me to some consideration, at least?'

'You had sex with me because you wanted to,' he pointed out ruthlessly. 'We both gave each other pleasure, which is what sex is all about. It's as simple as that, and if you try to read any more into it then you're just deluding yourself.'

She eyed him with an icy bitterness, then nodded. 'Yes. You're right, Fraser. I was deluding myself. I thought that for the first time in my life I'd met an honest, decent man. Someone I could really fall in love with. But I was wrong as usual, wasn't I? You might have the good looks and the wealth and the position but you're nothing more than a cynical, heartless brute.'

With a contemptuous toss of her head she headed for the door but he held out a restraining arm, barring her way. The firelight reflected in his eyes and played menacingly over the harsh angles of his face. 'You've just managed to spoil what—up till now—could have been a truly memorable evening.'

Her mouth gaped in outrage. 'Me? *I've* spoilt it?'

'Yes, you. You and your damned jealousy.'

'Jealous?' she echoed. 'Me...jealous?' She gave a scathing laugh. 'You're imagining things.'

'Then why did you ask about Pamela?' he challenged. 'If it isn't jealousy then why should you care how many other women I know?'

There was an uncomfortably cold logic behind his accusation and she muttered, 'I...I told you. I stupidly imagined that I was...was...' Her voice stumbled to an awkward halt and she compressed her lips in angry silence.

'That you were falling in love with me,' he finished drily. 'Well, I'm extremely flattered but just because I find you sexually exciting don't let it go to your head. You haven't yet earned the exclusive rights to my time or affections. Until I offer you the chance to become the First Lady of this Clan I'll see and go with anyone I damn well please.'

In a voice of fury she grated, 'That's just fine by me, Mr Fraser of Suilvach, just so long as you remember that I'm off-limits to you from now on. Now, move that damned arm and let me pass.'

Misty-eyed with rage and heartache, she slammed the library door behind her and stumbled upstairs to her room.

A night of broken, troubled sleep left her with a heavy head in the morning and she brought herself back to life under a hot then cold shower.

For convenience and comfort she donned a pale blue jogging-suit and trainers, then threw the window open and took half a dozen deep breaths. The bright, clear dawn smelt of the sea and aromatic pine resin and beyond the trees she could see the surf breaking on the beach.

The feeling of anger and injustice which had made her toss and turn all night had gone, leaving in its place an odd mixture of guilt and regret. At least she could now be honest enough with herself to admit that she'd been in the wrong and that she'd given Fraser sufficient justification for being annoyed at her.

Ever since she'd arrived here she'd been making it vociferously clear to him that she wasn't his fiancée and that she had no intention whatsoever of marrying him. In those circumstances she'd had no right mentioning Pamela.

Her tongue had vigorously denied his charge of jealousy but her heart knew better, and now she knew with sickening clarity that she'd made the classic female mistake of equating sex with love when everyone knew that men were merely driven by the urge to prove their dominance and masculinity. Could it really be possible that she'd allowed herself to fall in love with that unfathomable enigma of a man? Well, it certainly looked that way, because why else would she be standing here making excuses for him?

This, of course, was going to make things a damned sight more awkward than they had been. She didn't belong here and they both knew it. He was merely putting up with her in consideration of the feelings the locals had towards Kirsty and the legend and God knew what else but, when it came to the crunch, he'd ditch her and marry the woman he really wanted.

With shoulders slumped in dejection she turned from the window, made up her bed, then ventured downstairs.

In the hallway she paused, listening for sounds of activity, but the house was quiet. Impulsively she opened the front door, closed it gently behind her and made her way through the trees towards the beach. At the water's edge she stopped and stood indecisively while a couple of gulls wheeled curiously overhead. To her left the beach led round the bay towards the village and, making up her mind at last, she began a fast trot in the other direction.

It was heavy-going through the wet sand and after two hundred yards she found her lungs labouring for air. She slowed down to a walk for the next fifty yards to regain her breath, then began running again. After ten minutes of alternate walking and jogging she rounded the northern tip of the bay. Her green eyes widened in wonder and she perched herself on a rock to contemplate the view ahead. Never had she seen anything so hauntingly, breathtakingly beautiful as this. Green rollers from the Atlantic crashing upon mile after mile of blinding white sand...massive dunes creating suntraps between themselves and the towering, red granite cliffs. It looked like some Utopia, untouched as yet by the grimy finger of civilisation. This was the kind of place God had created for poets in search of inspiration, or troubled souls in search of peace.

Perhaps it was the sight of all that loneliness and beauty, or perhaps it was just the way she was feeling, but something suspiciously like a tear trickled from the corner of one eye and glistened on her cheek. Lost in her thoughts and unaware of time passing she sat on the rock until at last she gave a sigh, got to her feet, and began retracing her steps to the house.

The exercise had at least given her an appetite and the smell of grilled bacon lured her towards the kitchen. Halfway along the passage she heard the low murmur of Fraser's voice and she hesitated. The prospect of facing up to him this early in the day wasn't something she relished, but on the other hand it had to be done sooner or later so she was as well to get it over with now. Mustering the tattered remains of her self-confidence, she took a deep breath and made her entrance.

'Good morning, Mrs MacKay.'

The housekeeper turned from the cooker and smiled. 'I was just coming up to wake you. Help yourself to orange juice and cereal and I'll cook you something nice.'

Uncomfortably aware of Fraser's speculative eye on her she poured some milk and cornflakes into a bowl, then seated herself across the table from him. He sipped his coffee, then sat back in his seat and commented drily, 'You're looking very athletic this morning, Avalon. Are you going for a run?'

'I've already been,' she murmured, annoyed at the faint note of sarcasm in his voice. 'I got up an hour ago and went for a jog along the beach.'

He looked suitably impressed and nodded in approval. 'Good. A good few lungfuls of fresh sea-air will do you a power of good. Did you sleep well last night?'

'Like a log,' she lied.

'Aye. It must have been all that hectic activity you indulged in last night.' He smiled at her innocently, then raised his voice for the housekeeper's benefit. 'Avalon really let herself go last night, Mrs MacKay. It was her very first time but she soon got into the rhythm. I think she enjoyed it so much she could have gone on all night.'

She spluttered over her cornflakes and stared across the table at him in horror.

'Oh, aye? And what was she doing, then?' the housekeeper queried.

His blue eyes gleamed with devilment and Avalon's heart froze. He wouldn't . . . he couldn't! Fraser tilted an eyebrow at her, then chuckled. 'An eightsome reel. I told her not to but she insisted on taking part.'

Very funny, Avalon thought furiously. She glared at him for a moment longer, then attacked her corn-flakes again.

Fraser poured himself some more coffee, then said, 'Don't bother about lunch for us, Mrs MacKay. Avalon and I will have a meal at the hotel. We probably won't be back until late afternoon.'

'Well, if you're going through to Inverness you could fetch back some——'

'Not today, Mrs MacKay. I'm taking the *Flamingo* up to the salmon cages in Larig Bay.' He grinned at Avalon. 'You don't mind taking a little boat trip, do you?'

Would it make any difference if she did? she asked herself resentfully. Considering how her last boat trip had turned out it wasn't exactly top of her list of fun activities. Pushing her empty bowl aside, she gave him a wintry smile. 'Anything you say, Fraser. Just so long as I'm not in your way.'

He gave a thin smile. 'Of course you won't be in my way, darling. In fact I insist that you come along.'

'Well, in that case . . . darling . . . how can I refuse?' The loaded sarcasm in her voice was lost on Mrs MacKay, who sighed and smiled happily at this display of light-hearted banter between two lovers.

It was two hours later when they drove into the village and parked by the harbour. The *Flamingo* was a launch with an enclosed cockpit and the sleek, powerful lines of a thoroughbred. Fraser stood on the edge of the jetty, staring down at it fondly and giving Avalon an enthusiastic description of its pedigree and performance.

She listened with an air of distant politeness, nodding at all the appropriate places, then she finally interrupted with, 'How far is it to where we're going?'

'About twenty miles down the coast.'

She gave him a withering look. 'You're taking me twenty miles to look at some fish?'

'Why not?'

'Well, to tell the truth, I'm not that interested in fish.'

He frowned in displeasure. 'Well, that's too bad. The future wife of the Chief should be interested in everything to do with the estate.'

So he was still going through with this charade, was he? She bit her lip in frustration then said quietly, 'Look, Fraser . . . We're alone here and there's no one to overhear us so let's stop the pretence, shall we? You don't really want to marry me so we needn't bother with all this nonsense.'

His lips tightened in anger, then his fingers dug painfully into her shoulders and his voice cracked like a whip. 'You haven't got the faintest idea what I really want, you little fool. But whether I marry you or not is entirely up to you.'

Her green eyes stared up at him defiantly. 'Oh, yes. Your wife has to be someone worthy of the position. I was forgetting. Silly me. I always thought that marriage had more to do with love than anything else.'

His fingers loosened their grip but there was no escape from his coldly penetrating eyes as he growled, 'So far you've been doing just fine. Don't let that touchy temper of yours spoil everything.'

'I haven't got a temper,' she muttered angrily. 'At least I didn't have until I met you.'

'You weren't a real woman, either, until you met me,' he reminded her acidly. 'But you're learning fast. There's hope for you yet.'

She supposed that was his idea of a compliment. 'All right.' She sighed. 'Let's go and visit your precious fish.'

'Not yet.' He glanced at his watch. 'I've got some accounts to go over at the harbour office. Meet me there in an hour then we'll have some lunch at the hotel before we leave.'

She looked at him in exasperation. 'And what am I supposed to do for the next hour on my own?' she demanded. 'Sit on the wall and twiddle my thumbs?'

'No,' he said heavily. 'What you're supposed to do is show a bit of initiative and self-confidence—not to mention sociability. There are plenty of people walking about. They already know who you are and they'll stop and chat with you at the drop of a hat. At least try and pretend that you're interested in them and their way of life.'

She opened her mouth in protest but he'd already turned his back on her and was striding off purpose-

fully towards the low wooden building. For a moment
she stood, clenching her fists in anger, then with an
explosive sigh of exasperation she made her way back
along the jetty. Just what exactly had he meant by
that last remark? Was he accusing her of being some
sort of bigoted snob? Of course she was interested in
the people. She was interested in everyone. She'd
always tried her best to be friendly with strangers, no
matter who they were. That was her trouble. She could
be too friendly at times. Too naïve and trusting. Too
easily duped and taken advantage of.

When she reached the main street she looked both
ways indecisively, trying to make up her mind. There
wasn't even a café where she could sit down and have
a coffee. Even the hotel bar wasn't open yet.

Smiling inanely at the passers-by, but unable to
think of a plausible excuse for stopping them going
about their lawful business in order to chat and pass
the time, she realised that this was the second time
Fraser had put her in this situation. He'd done the
same thing at the party last night but Aileen had
spotted her and come to her rescue.

Suddenly the answer was there. The cottage up on
the hill! She'd go and talk to Kirsty. She'd intended
visiting her, anyway, and getting the answers to a few
questions that were still puzzling her, and right now
was the ideal opportunity.

The front door of the cottage was open and at her
tentative knock the familiar lilting voice sang out,
'Come in, Avalon.'

As she stepped into the room Kirsty was already
pouring tea into two mugs on the table and again
Avalon felt that odd little shiver. 'How...how did
you know it was me at the door, Kirsty?'

'I was out in the garden a few minutes ago. I saw you heading up the hill.'

'Oh . . .' Avalon smiled, feeling foolish.

Kirsty surveyed her with a kindly expression. 'Those jogging-suits look nice and comfortable. Do you think they make them to suit a figure like mine?' Without waiting for an answer she chuckled. 'I doubt it. I'll stick to jumpers and my old tweed skirt.' She paused and put her head to one side as she looked deeply into Avalon's eyes, then she smiled again and gave a little nod of satisfaction. 'Aye . . . There's something different about you, Avalon. You've changed.'

'Changed?' she asked cautiously. 'In what way?'

'Well . . . let's just say that you seem a little more grown-up.' She chuckled again. 'Now, don't start feeling embarrassed. I've seen that glow in other girls' eyes many a time. They don't know it's there but I can see it.' She pulled a chair out. 'Now, just sit down, drink your tea and tell me what's troubling you.'

'What . . . what makes you think there's anything troubling me?' It couldn't be as obvious as that, surely?

'Aye . . . Well, if you say so. Where's Fraser?'

'Down at the harbour going over some accounts.'

Kirsty nodded. 'And you just took the chance to pay a social call. Well, that's nice.' She opened her battered old tobacco tin and rolled a cigarette. 'I hear you were at the party last night. Did you enjoy yourself?'

'Yes, I did,' Avalon admitted. 'I didn't think I would but I had a great time. People here really know how to enjoy themselves.'

Kirsty laughed. 'Aye. Any excuse for a good drink and a dance, that's us.' She lit her cigarette and blew the smoke at the ceiling. 'I'm glad everything is working out fine for you and Fraser. He can be a bit stubborn at times but he's a good man. None better.'

This was getting her nowhere, Avalon thought. Putting her cup down firmly, she took a deep breath and said, 'I lied. There is something troubling me. I'm trying my best to understand what's going on here, Kirsty. I came here because I think you're the only one who can give me the answers I want.'

Kirsty gave a sympathetic smile. 'It's only natural that you're confused. I said you'd need time to settle down.'

Avalon sighed. 'It has nothing to do with settling down. One of the things I don't understand is this— if Fraser really wants to get married, why doesn't he choose a local girl? He's certainly got plenty to pick from. I saw that at the party last night ... Girls a lot prettier and more used to the ways up here than I am.'

Kirsty smiled. 'Is that all you're worried about? I thought you knew. His bride has to come from the sea. She has to——'

Avalon shook her head impatiently. 'Please don't start lecturing me about legends and fairies and stuff like that. I know about his mother and his grand-mother but it seems to me more likely to be coincidence.'

There was an awkward silence, then Kirsty said quietly, 'Fraser can't marry anyone who is related to the Clan. He has to marry an outsider. It's a Clan law that was made hundreds of years ago.' Seeing the look of scepticism on Avalon's face, she hastened to explain. 'We're only a small Clan in this part of the country. In their wisdom, our distant forefathers de-creed that all future Clan Chiefs had to marry an outsider. The new bloodlines would make for sound, healthy stock.' She offered a tentative smile. 'To us it's always been common sense.'

Avalon stared at her, digesting this piece of information in silence, then she said grimly, 'There's something you forgot to mention, isn't there? Something about the girl having to be worthy of the position. He's forever telling me about it.'

'But . . . but of course you're worthy! I can tell by the——'

'Fraser doesn't think so,' she interrupted coldly. 'Or at least he has serious doubts. I don't think he has any intention of marrying me, Kirsty.'

The older woman's eyes widened in shock. 'How can you say such a thing? Of course he'll marry you. All he's worried about is——'

'Who's this girl Pamela I keep hearing about?'

'Pamela?'

'Yes. Pamela,' she repeated impatiently. 'There's nothing to stop him marrying her, is there?'

Suddenly Kirsty pressed her hand to her forehead and groaned as if she was having a blinding headache. For a second Avalon thought it was merely a trick to avoid answering the question, then she saw the pallor on Kirsty's face and she reached out in concern. 'Kirsty? What's wrong? Look . . . I didn't meant to upset you.'

'I . . . I'm all right.' There was a slightly dazed look in Kirsty's eyes and she managed a weak smile. 'I take these spells now and again. What . . . what were we talking about?'

'It doesn't matter. Just you relax and I'll pour some fresh tea.'

'No. I remember now. You wanted to know about Pamela.' She seemed undecided then she queried, 'Have you asked Fraser about her?'

'Yes. He told me to mind my own business.'

Kirsty nodded thoughtfully. 'I see. Well, if he didn't want to discuss Pamela with you then he must have a good reason, and if that's the case I don't think I should...should...' Her voice trailed away and her eyes grew large, staring into the distance.

This time Avalon got to her feet in alarm. 'Kirsty?' she queried. There was a thin film of perspiration on Kirsty's brow and her fists, clenched on the table before her, were white-knuckled with tension. Dashing round the table, she leaned down and stared into the sightless eyes. 'Kirsty? Shall I fetch a doctor?' What could it be? she wondered desperately. Some sort of fit? Should she try and get Kirsty to lie down? Racked with a feeling of utter helplessness she again wondered guiltily if she'd somehow been the cause of this. A reaction to stress brought on by her questioning, perhaps?

'Kirsty?' she pleaded. 'Talk to me. Please say something.' She placed her fingers gently on the older woman's wrist and felt the wildly erratic pulse. She would have to get help. This could be the start of a stroke.

Suddenly she almost jumped out of her skin as Kirsty said in a strange, hoarse-sounding voice, 'The *Starling* ... It's in danger. Tell Fraser...'

Avalon bit her lip in anguish. Was the woman starting to rave now? 'It...it's all right,' she said soothingly. 'Just you take it easy and I'll fetch...'

Kirsty's hand reached out and gripped her arm painfully. 'You must hurry. *Starling* ... Seven Needles ... Tell Fraser.'

'He ... he's down at the harbour.'

'Yes ... yes. For God's sake, lassie! Hurry!'

Avalon didn't waste any more time arguing. The urgency in Kirsty's voice finally galvanised her into action and she hurried to the door then, with one final, doubtful look at Kirsty, she began running down the hill towards the village.

Four minutes later, gasping for breath, she burst into the harbour office. At her sudden, explosive entrance Fraser got to his feet, a dark frown on his face. 'What the devil ... ?' She slumped in front of him drawing in great lungfuls of air. Grabbing her shoulders, he said gently, 'Take your time, Avalon. Don't be frightened. You're safe now.'

'It ... it isn't me,' she gulped. 'Kirsty ... Some sort of fit... I've to tell you...*Starling*... Danger. Seven... Seven something.'

'Seven Needles?'

She nodded. 'I don't know what it means ...' From the grim expression on his face it obviously meant something to him and he swore under his breath.

'Right. I'll need help. A life may be at stake. Will you come with me or do I have to waste time looking for someone else?'

She met his challenge indignantly. 'If you knew me as well as you think you do you wouldn't ask a stupid question like that. Let's go.'

CHAPTER SIX

THE *Flamingo's* engine started with a roar and Fraser
headed her at full throttle out of the harbour. Spray
blotted out visibility and he flicked on the wipers to
clear the cockpit screen, then he beckoned Avalon
closer so that she could hear his voice over the noise.
'You'll find a coil of rope in the locker behind you.
Get it out. We may be needing it.'

She did as she was told, then shouted back at him,
'Would you mind telling me what's going on? Whose
life is in danger?'

'Big Duncan,' Fraser yelled back. 'He fishes for
lobsters. The *Starling* is his boat and if it's being swept
on to the Seven Needles it'll be smashed into
matchwood. It'll take us about ten minutes to get
there. I hope we're not too late. Big Duncan can't
swim.'

She looked at him thoughtfully... at the tense lines
of his jaw and his mouth...his aggressive, wide-legged
stance at the wheel. Like a hot-blooded man who
thrived on challenge he looked ready and willing to
sail into the very jaws of hell, dragging her with him.
She tugged at his arm to attract his attention again
and said, 'Is there a radio on board the *Starling*?
Could he have called anyone for help?'

'No. I told you. It's only a small lobster boat.'

Her lips formed another question, then she thought
better of it. She'd find out for herself soon enough.
If there was no boat and no sign of wreckage when

they got there then Kirsty's warning could be dismissed as the ravings of an eccentric old woman. But on the other hand...

Fraser was the first to spot it and he headed straight for the notorious reef. As the distance rapidly shortened she could see the rollers breaking and foaming over the outcrop of jagged rocks. A man in a yellow oilskin was standing up in the frail craft, desperately fending off the danger with a long pole.

'His engine must have cut out,' Fraser told her grimly. 'This is going to be damned awkward. I'll have to tow him in reverse or the rope may foul our propeller.' He cut the throttle until the engine was idling and allowed the *Flamingo* to edge within fifteen feet of the *Starling*. In order to maintain position he had to keep constantly juggling with the rudder and the engine in slow reverse. The noise wasn't so bad and he rapidly explained the situation. 'I can't leave the wheel or the current will drive us on to the reef. This is the closest I can get.' His blue eyes studied her doubtfully. 'You'll have to do the rest on your own. I suppose I can depend on you not to do something stupid like falling overboard?'

'I can only do my best,' she snapped. 'Just keep your sarcastic remarks to yourself and tell me what you want.'

He pointed through the windscreen. 'Take the rope and fasten one end to the cleat at the bow. When you've done that, coil the rope and throw it to Duncan so that he can fasten it to the stern of the *Starling*.'

She shrugged. 'No problem. You don't have to worry about me. I can look after myself.'

'Then stop chattering and get on with it,' he growled.

Grabbing the coil of rope, she clambered out of the cockpit and stood erect on the pitching deck. Getting her balance, she carefully walked forward towards the bow, then she knelt down and tied one end of the rope to the big brass cleat. Making sure it was tight, she raised herself to her feet again, holding the remainder of the rope coiled in one hand. If she missed she'd have to drag the rope back out of the water and recoil it and try again. But every second was precious. She couldn't afford to miss.

She heard Fraser yell from the cockpit. 'Throw the damned thing, will you? We haven't got all bloody day.'

She ignored him and patiently waited for the right moment. As the bows of the *Flamingo* rose and dipped in the swell she waited until it had risen as far as it would go, then she drew her arm back and hurled the rope across the watery chasm. It sailed through the air and landed almost at Duncan's feet.

With a feeling of triumph she acknowledged his quick wave then tentatively made her way back to the cockpit and grinned at Fraser. 'Satisfied?'

'Aye . . .' he acknowledged with a strained smile. 'You did well, but Duncan's still in trouble.'

Mystified, she poked her head up and saw what Fraser meant. Although the rope was still at Duncan's feet the *Starling* was only inches from the jagged rocks, and it was taking all Duncan's attention with the pole to stave off disaster.

'He isn't getting the time to tie it!' she cried. 'Why doesn't he forget about the *Starling*, grab the rope and let us pull him on board?'

'Because he's a stubborn cuss and won't leave his boat to be sunk, that's why,' muttered Fraser. He eyed her doubtfully once more. 'I'll need to leave you in charge of the *Flamingo* for a few minutes.'

Her eyes widened in disbelief and she stared at him. 'What do you mean, leave me in charge? I can't handle this boat! Especially not when the engine is in reverse. You just said yourself that you couldn't leave the wheel or we'd end up on the rocks.'

He acknowledged her argument with a reluctant nod, then said gravely, 'I know. But we haven't got any choice, Avalon. I'll have to swim over there and secure the rope for him.' He let go the wheel and she made a grab for it as he began peeling off his shirt.

The *Flamingo* was starting to swing and she turned the wheel frantically. Now they were swinging the other way as she overcorrected and she yelled at him, 'I can't do it!'

'Yes, you can. Just remember to keep the throttle wide enough to——'

'I tell you, I can't!' she shouted angrily. He ignored her and as he began kicking off his shoes she gave a cry of exasperation and dashed past him.

'What the . . . ?' He made a desperate grab for her but she dodged, leapt up on to the deck, and launched herself over the side. There were times when you just had to take things into your own hands and this was one of them.

She broke surface, spluttering and gasping at the cold, then struck out strongly towards the *Starling*.

The look on Duncan's face was one of utter amazement as she hauled herself up and over the side to land in a sodden heap among the lobster pots at his feet. There was no time to spare for introductions and she scrabbled to her knees, grabbed the rope and

hitched it around the rudder post. Only then did she
get to her feet and wave a signal to Fraser.

The *Flamingo* increased power, backed away in reverse, taking up the slack in the tow rope, then she
felt the *Starling* move as it was pulled clear of the
rocks.

'Thank God for that,' gasped Duncan as he dropped
the pole. He stared at her for a moment in wonder,
then he grinned. 'You must be the *caileagh bhan*
everyone is talking about. It's a lucky man I am that
you and Fraser turned up just as that clapped-out old
engine packed in.'

The cold was penetrating to her very bones now,
and she hugged herself. 'You say that the engine broke
down just before we arrived?'

'Aye. Well . . . no more than two or three minutes.'

She shivered and gave him an awkward smile. 'Well,
you're safe now. That's all that matters.'

They were about two hundred yards clear of the
reef when Fraser cut the *Flamingo's* engine and waited
until the *Starling* had drifted alongside. He reached
down with his hand and as she took it he pulled her
unceremoniously aboard before turning his attention
to Duncan.

'Are you all right, Duncan?'

'I'm fine, Fraser,' the fisherman called up. 'The
bloody engine has seized up, though. Sounds like a
broken crankshaft.'

'Right. I'll tow you back to harbour but I'm not
going to do it in reverse. I'll transfer the rope from
the bow to the stern but we'll have to keep it short
and clear of the prop.'

Avalon shivered again and felt in imminent danger
of turning an unhealthy dark blue colour. By the time

she'd found a blanket in the emergency locker, and draped it around her shoulders, the new towing arrangements had been made and they were on their way back to the harbour.

As soon as Fraser had set the course he turned and confronted her angrily. 'If I had the time right now I'd put you over my knee and leather some damned sense into you. That was a crazy thing to do.'

She eyed him in defiant silence and he went on with his harangue. 'What the hell is the matter with you? Have you got some mad compulsion to jump into the sea and drown yourself?'

'I didn't drown, did I?' she pointed out calmly.

'No. But you easily could have. There's a strong current around the Seven Needles. You saw the way the *Starling* was being pushed on to the rocks.'

'Oh, stop moaning,' she said crossly. 'If you could see further than your own injured pride you'd realise that I did the only sensible thing possible in the circumstances.'

'Sensible!' he scoffed. 'You don't know the meaning of the word.'

It was too much for her and she reared up. 'I told you that I couldn't handle the *Flamingo* but would you listen? Oh, no! Not you.'

'You could at least have tried,' he retorted.

'What good would that have been?' she demanded. 'I might have tried and failed and run the *Flamingo* into the reef. Then we'd all have drowned, wouldn't we?' She gave him one final glare. 'I wasn't being stupid . . . or brave. I was being practical.'

Instead of answering her he gave another snort, then scowled ahead through the windscreen.

Wearily she removed her trainers and emptied the water out of them on to the floor, aware that he was watching her from the corner of his eye. If he started arguing with her again she'd . . . she'd hit him over the head with something very heavy.

Suddenly he grunted at her. 'Are you cold?'

'Of course I'm cold,' she snapped. 'I'm freezing. The water up here isn't exactly lukewarm, is it?'

'Then you'd better come and stand next to me. I don't want you catching pneumonia.'

'I didn't know you cared,' she muttered.

He turned to look at her and said quietly, 'I do. Much more than you think.'

It wasn't just the way he'd said it . . . You could lie with your voice but never with your eyes and there was a look in his that put an extra beat in her heart. She moved closer and he put an arm around her shoulders. 'Snuggle into me as close as you can, Avalon.'

Needing no second invitation she pressed herself against the heat of his body and murmured up at him, 'I'm soaking wet. Perhaps you'll be the one to get pneumonia.'

He gave a crooked grin. 'I wouldn't mind. We could lie in bed and sweat it out together.'

She trembled a little. Now there was a thought. Already she could feel a sneeze coming on.

The hotel bar was open and that was the first place Fraser made for as soon as the *Flamingo* was safely tied up in the harbour. Ordering a large glass of whisky with hot water and lemon, he thrust it into her hand. 'Drink that slowly while I organise some dry clothes for you.'

Avalon took it gratefully and managed to stop her teeth chattering long enough to take a large sip. The few customers who were already in were eyeing her with a curiosity which immediately turned to awed admiration as Fraser quickly explained to them what had happened.

She began to flush with embarrassment at all the attention and she chided him quietly. 'Look... You shouldn't make such a big deal of what I did. You make me sound like...'

'I'm merely giving them the straight story before Duncan arrives,' he explained with amused patience. 'If we leave it up to him he'll have all these people believing you can part the Red Sea.'

Calling the landlord from the other end of the bar, he gave him a list of orders regarding fresh clothes for her and a room and bath being made available, then he led her to a table next to the crackling log fire.

When they were seated she leaned towards him conspiratorially and said in a quiet voice, 'When I was in Duncan's boat he told me that his engine had stopped just a few minutes before we reached him. He wasn't in any danger at all until then.'

Fraser simply shrugged. 'I guessed as much.'

She waited on him to elaborate on his statement, then queried in an impatient whisper, 'Is that all you've got to say? Don't you realise what it means?'

'Yes...' he drawled. 'But if you're asking me how Kirsty knew about it before it happened, then I can't help you. She knew you were coming before you arrived and I can't explain that, either. No one can, so there's little point in worrying about it.'

His matter-of-fact tone and expression said it all. You either believed in the supernatural or you didn't. She'd put down the story of Kirsty's 'gift' as superstitious nonsense but she'd just witnessed it in action for herself. It was time to have a rethink. Not just about Kirsty, but all the other things—the legend...the fairy guardians...the Fire Magic...

No, she told herself shakily. She wasn't going to delve any deeper into things that had no answer. It was safer to let it be.

'Feeling any better?' Fraser asked, watching her closely.

She took another sip of her drink. There was something different about him, she thought. The angles and planes of his face weren't quite so unremittingly harsh...the set of his mouth was not so grim. His confrontational aggressiveness had been replaced by concern and a certain air of puzzled respect. Perhaps it wasn't quite love but, for the present, it was enough. She looked deeply into those laser-blue eyes, smiled and murmured, 'I feel good. In fact, I feel very good.'

'You'll feel even better after a hot bath.' He contemplated her with wry amusement, then grinned. 'I think we'll forget about visiting the salmon cages for the time being. There's a bit of a mermaid about you and you'll probably find some other excuse for diving overboard.'

She'd barely finished her drink when Aileen appeared breathlessly with a new jogging-suit, trainers and underwear and, at a signal from Fraser, the landlord came over and presented him with a room key. 'Number three is vacant, Fraser. And I've made sure there's plenty of hot water.'

Fraser escorted her upstairs into the room, laid the fresh clothes on the bed, then ran the bath. 'Have a nice long, relaxing bath,' he said. 'Then we'll have lunch. How does that sound?'

'Perfect,' she murmured, the tiny catch in her voice betraying her quickening pulse as that hungry look came back into his eyes again.

Putting his hands on her slim waist, he looked down at her with a smouldering yearning. 'I don't know how you do it, Avalon. Even in a soggy old jogging-suit you radiate like a thousand-watt bulb.'

'Well, if you keep looking at me like that you're going to blow my fuse,' she said huskily. 'Don't you think you should go downstairs, now?'

He sighed, then grinned. 'Aye. I think I should. What I've got in mind isn't what you'd call relaxing. I'll postpone it until a more suitable time.'

As soon as he'd made his reluctant departure she peeled off her wet clothes, dumped them in the laundry bag, then climbed into the bath and lowered herself blissfully into the warm water.

Pink and glowing and wearing the new all-black jogging-suit, she made her way down to the bar half an hour later to find the place crowded. At the sight of her the loud buzz of conversation died away and a path was cleared for her as she made her way in some embarrassment towards Fraser, who was standing at the bar. His blue eyes looked her up and down with quiet approval and he murmured, 'I warned you that news travels fast around here. While you were having your bath Duncan was inviting half the village here to drink your health.'

She bit her lip and looked up at him imploringly. 'Look . . . I get nervous when everyone keeps looking at me. Can't we go somewhere else where it's not . . . ?'

He shook his head. 'This is their way of saying thank you for saving Duncan.'

'If they want to thank anyone it should be Kirsty,' she whispered fiercely. 'All I did was——'

A loud voice shouted from the back of the crowd. 'Why don't you give the lassie a kiss, Fraser? Then we can all get down to the business of drinking her health in earnest.'

Fraser grinned and replied loudly, 'That's just what I'm going to do, as soon as she closes her mouth long enough to give me a chance.' As he pulled her closer his face hovered over hers and he grinned in anticipation, then growled, 'Don't worry. This is for my pleasure, not theirs.' Suddenly he claimed her half-parted lips with his own and, through the thudding of her heart, she heard the crowd cheering their approval. The kiss went on and on, demanding yet tender, sending delicious tremors to the very soles of her feet.

The taste of him lingered tantalisingly as he finally released her and murmured in her ear, 'While we're talking about saving lives, the man who saved yours is here.'

She had to think for a moment, then she raised her eyebrows. 'The man on the tractor who found me?'

'Aye. Old Gavin.' He beckoned to someone further along the bar and a moment later she found herself confronted by an unassuming man in his sixties wearing starched overalls and an ancient, oil-stained deerstalker hat.

She offered him a friendly smile. 'You must be Gavin, the tractor-driver who found me.'

'Aye, miss...' He removed his hat in a gesture of respect. 'That's me. Gave me a real turn when I saw you lying on the rocks.'

She stepped closer, took his hand, and shook it. 'I'm sorry about that. But if it wasn't for you I wouldn't be standing here now.' She turned to Fraser and said crisply, 'Don't just stand there. Buy my friend a drink. A very large one.'

Fraser grinned. 'Talisker, isn't it, Gavin?'

'Aye,' said the old man happily. 'I think I could manage a wee sensation...'

Fraser ordered a double of Gavin's favourite whisky, then drew her aside confidentially. 'There's been someone patiently waiting to see you outside for the last fifteen minutes. I want you to go out and talk to him.'

She gave him a puzzled frown. 'Who is it?'

'An admirer.'

She looked at him closely. 'This is some kind of joke, isn't it?'

He shrugged as if the whole thing had nothing to do with him and grunted. 'No. It seems that you're gaining a certain popularity around here.'

'Well, I'm not interested in being popular,' she muttered. 'People begin to expect too much from you.'

'Everything has a price,' he grunted. 'Now go and talk to him. He's waited long enough.'

'Why doesn't he come inside?' she demanded.

'Because he's too embarrassed,' he replied drily. 'Now, either you go and put him out of his misery or I'll carry you out bodily.'

'All right . . .' she grumbled. 'Don't start getting all macho again. I'll go.' Completely mystified and a little nervous at what she was getting herself into, she made her way through the crowded bar and out of the front door.

There was no one at all outside and she'd just decided that it was a joke in pretty poor taste when a small boy detached himself from a recess in the wall and approached her shyly.

She recognised the freckled face and red hair immediately. They belonged to the boy who had been sent by Kirsty to get her plimsolls from the harbour store. Was this her admirer? She hid her surprise behind an open friendly smile of recognition. 'Hello. You're Jamie, aren't you? Did you want to see me?'

He shuffled his feet for a moment then brought a box of chocolates from behind his back and thrust it at her. 'This is for you. A . . . a present. I . . . I bought it with my pocket money.'

Her eyes widened in astonishment. 'For me? That . . . that's very kind of you, Jamie. But you really shouldn't have bothered.' This was getting out of hand, she thought. It was one thing for the locals to toast her health over a glass of whisky but when the kids started spending their pocket money on her . . . 'Look, Jamie . . .' she said awkwardly. 'You really shouldn't . . . I mean . . .'

He shuffled his feet some more and said diffidently, 'I wanted to. My dad told me how you swam to his boat and helped him off the Seven Needles.'

Suddenly it dawned on her. 'Oh! I see. You're Big Duncan's son?'

'Aye. If . . . if you don't like the chocolates I can take them back and change them for something else.'

She swallowed the sudden lump that came to her throat. She felt like hugging him but, knowing what little boys could be like, he'd probably take to his heels in embarrassment. 'They're my favourites,' she assured him gravely. 'I'll keep them for later.'

He grinned in relief. 'Aye... Well... I'll get away now.'

As he turned to skip off she held out her hand. 'No... Hold on a minute, Jamie.' She'd had a sudden idea. 'I'd like to ask you a favour.' Glancing around to see that no one was watching, she leaned down and whispered in his ear.

His eyes widened as he listened to her request, then he grinned. 'Aye. I can do that. It's easy.' He shuffled his feet for a moment, then added quietly, 'Anyway... Kirsty says that you're very special and that we've all got to do everything we can to help you.'

Avalon took his hand in hers and led him over to the harbour wall. 'Let's sit down for five minutes and we'll talk about it.'

Fraser was leaning against the far end of the bar, deep in conversation with Kirsty, when she went back inside and Kirsty greeted her arrival with a smile. 'They've been telling me what a brave girl you were, Avalon.' Her brown eyes twinkled for a moment, then she turned to Fraser. 'Will you look at her! The poor wee thing is shy. Her cheeks are all pink.'

'How's your headache?' she asked politely. 'Better now?'

Kirsty raised a glass of whisky and chuckled. 'Aye. I feel as fresh as a daisy.'

'I'm glad to hear it.' She laid the box of chocolates on the bar and sighed. 'These are a present from young Jamie. He bought them for me. It isn't right. It was probably a whole week's pocket money.'

'Don't worry about it,' Fraser said easily. 'I'll put a few odd jobs his way. That'll more than make it up to him.'

His thoughtfulness and generosity touched her but she still felt uncomfortable. 'That's very kind of you,' she said awkwardly. 'But I think you're missing the point. Both of you are.' She saw the frown on Fraser's face and she said heatedly, 'Everyone here thinks I'm something special. Jamie just told me.'

'But you are special,' Kirsty said quietly. 'You're very special.'

'I'm not,' she maintained fiercely. 'And you're the one to blame, Kirsty. I know you mean well but you've got these people believing all sorts of things about me.'

Kirsty's face crumpled and she looked at Fraser in perplexity, but he put his hand on her shoulder and said gently, 'I think you should leave Avalon and I to discuss this between ourselves, Kirsty.'

'Aye . . .' Kirsty bit her lip then she summoned up a smile. 'But everything will turn out right in the end, Fraser. My . . . my friends said that it would and they're never wrong.'

As Kirsty dejectedly made her departure Avalon felt a sharp pang of guilt, and from the thunderous look on Fraser's face she knew she was in for a stormy time. Resisting the urge to run after Kirsty and apologise, she turned to Fraser and got her thrust in first. 'Well! You heard her, didn't you? She's still on about her damned fairies and how they'll make everything all right.'

'You were completely out of order, talking to her like that,' he retorted with barely controlled anger.

She remembered only too vividly the warnings he'd given her about saying nothing to upset Kirsty or the locals but she was past caring. Ever since last night one thing had been dominating her mind. Her attempt to get an answer from Kirsty earlier on had been fruitless but now she was determined to get to the bottom of it, once and for all. Staring unflinchingly into those angry blue eyes, she said, 'All you're interested in is humouring Kirsty, while I'm left to carry the burden and go on with this stupid pretence.'

'What pretence?' he demanded grimly.

'Pretending to be your fiancée,' she snapped. 'Why don't you just admit to Kirsty and all the others that you intend marrying Pamela?'

He stiffened and narrowed his eyes. 'I've already told you that——'

She cut him off impatiently. 'Pamela is no concern of mine. Well, you're wrong, Fraser. I'm tired of being used as a pawn in this game between you and Kirsty. It's quite obvious to me that you were all set to marry Pamela until I turned up and threw a spanner in the works.'

His face grew bleak. 'Go on,' he prompted coldly. 'I want to know who you've been talking to. Who's been discussing Pamela behind my back?'

She refused to be cowed by his threatening manner. 'No one in particular, but from what I can gather Pamela is a fairly frequent visitor to the house. Now, she wouldn't keep coming here without a reason, would she? Someone must be going out of his way to make her feel welcome. I'm not stupid, Fraser. I can put two and two together as well as anyone.'

'Aye... And come up with five,' he muttered under his breath.

'Look...' she said tiredly. 'It was obvious right from the start. When you first saw me you were unpleasantly surprised. You told Kirsty that you had plans but she made you promise to look after me.' Her eyes challenged him. 'Your plans were to marry Pamela, weren't they? They still are. The only reason that you haven't got rid of me is because you're afraid of hurting Kirsty's feelings.'

His voice had a hard edge of mockery. 'Go on. It's fascinating to see the way your mind works.'

Her anger was almost spent now and in its place came a feeling of empty bitterness. 'I see that you're not even bothering to deny it,' she muttered defeatedly.

He shrugged and said smoothly, 'All right. I deny it. Does that make you feel any better?'

She looked into the depths of his eyes, then shook her head. 'It would if I believed you meant it.'

'So now I'm a liar as well?' he growled. 'Are you forgetting who you're talking to?'

'There isn't much chance of that,' she muttered rebelliously. 'You're forever reminding me.'

'And it looks as if I'll just have to keep reminding you. You're in no position to question anything I do.'

'That's what I'm complaining about,' she retorted. 'I'm just a pawn and I'd better not forget it.'

'You'd rather be a queen?' he asked with a sardonic grin.

'No. I just wish the game were over and done with and I could leave here.'

'And what will you do then?' he asked drily. 'Keep on running every time you're confronted by a problem? That's the story of your life, isn't it?'

She bit her lip and avoided his eye until he gripped her fiercely by the shoulders and growled, 'You're being a blind, stubborn little fool again. Has it never occurred to you that I might . . . ?' He paused, then scowled. 'No, dammit! I don't owe you any explanations. You're just going to have to trust me.'

'Trust you!' She eyed him with hot resentment. 'Why should I?'

'Because I'm asking you to.' He released the pressure on her shoulders, then said quietly, 'No relationship can flourish without trust and respect. These are the qualities I demand from any woman.'

'And here was I thinking it was sexual attraction that was top of your list,' she replied with mild sarcasm.

'Aye . . .' He gave a cynical twist to his lips. 'But being good at sex is only half the story. You're prepared to submit to me sexually but in nothing else. That isn't good enough. I've never had to argue or explain and defend my actions to anyone before and I don't intend starting with you. As I said, you're going to have to trust me. Don't ever ask me about Pamela again.'

'I was always led to believe that in a normal relationship men and women were equal partners who could sit down and discuss things in a civilised manner. You ask me to trust you when it's quite obvious that you don't trust me. You want to keep all your little secrets to yourself.'

'That's right,' he acknowledged openly. 'But ours isn't what you'd call a "normal" relationship, is it? We only met because of some weird twist of Fate.'

'Collision would be a more appropriate word,' she amended tartly.

He gave her a cold smile. 'Call it anything you like but it's up to us to make the best of it.' He paused and his blue eyes challenged her. 'Well? You'll have to tell me now. Do I get your trust or am I asking too much?'

She wanted to trust him—desperately. Her foolish heart was voting for a 'yes' but it was having a hard time convincing her head. She knew to her bitter cost what had happened in the past when she'd put her trust in others. It was true that Fraser was like no other man she'd ever met, but what did she actually know about him?

She looked into the depths of those blue eyes seeking an answer, then, for better or worse, she nodded, and said quietly, 'Yes, Fraser. I trust you. God help me if I'm wrong, but I trust you.'

CHAPTER SEVEN

AVALON had completely forgotten about the evening
dress Aileen had said she was going to order until it
arrived a week later. As usual she'd got up early, taken
her morning jog along the beach, showered and had
just finished her breakfast in the kitchen when Mrs
MacKay informed her that Fraser wanted to see her
in the library.

She looked at the housekeeper in surprise. Fraser
had been in Brussels for the last four days attending
an EEC conference on fishing policy. 'I thought he
wasn't due home until tomorrow.'

'You know what Fraser is like,' Mrs MacKay con-
fided. 'He hasn't any time for all those bureaucrats
with their forms and red tape. Like enough he'll have
terrified the life out of them and they got through the
agenda in double-quick time.' She poured herself a
cup of tea. 'Anyway, he got home about four o'clock
this morning and he's been working in the library ever
since.'

Avalon got to her feet, telling herself that there was
nothing to feel nervous about. When he'd first gone
away she'd enjoyed the sudden release from tension
but it had been short-lived and after two days she'd
actually found herself wishing he were back. Without
him life was definitely lacking in something. There
was so much she missed about him. His unpredict-
ability for one thing, and never knowing if she was
in for a scolding or a lingering, romantic kiss. On

balance his moments of sweet tenderness far outnumbered his moods of dark brooding, but you could never be quite sure. Like now ...

Outside the library she paused in front of a hall mirror, looked despairingly at her hair, decided there was nothing she could do about it, then knocked on the door before entering.

The tentative smile on her face vanished abruptly as she took in his drawn and haggard appearance that told its own tale of a grinding schedule and precious little sleep. He was sitting at his desk, writing out a report, and at her entrance he dropped his pen thankfully and gave her a weary smile. 'Hello, Avalon. I'd almost forgotten how delightful you always manage to look in the morning.'

Voicing her concern, she said, 'Never mind how I look. What on earth have they been doing to you? You look exhausted.'

He sighed. 'Aye ... Bloody civil servants! I'd like to get them in a boat in a force ten gale north of Shetland. That would wipe the smug smiles off their faces as they laid down their rules and regulations about fishing quotas.' He poured himself a large glass of malt whisky from the crystal decanter on the desk. 'There's nothing wrong with me that a large drink and a few hours' sleep won't put right.'

'Is there anything I can do to help?' she asked quickly. 'Copy out notes? I can do shorthand and take dictation.'

He gestured towards the long white cardboard box on the side-table. 'Your dress has arrived. The one you'll be wearing at the Grand Ceilidh. Try it on and see if it fits. If not it'll have to go back.'

She lifted the box, tucked it under her arm, and was halfway to the door when his voice stopped her in her tracks. 'Where are you going?'

Raising her eyebrows in surprise she told him, 'To my room, of course.'

Tired though he was, he still managed to get a gleam of devilish humour in his eyes. 'There's no reason for mock-modesty, Avalon. I'm well-acquainted with the delightful charms your body has to offer. Try it on here.'

'While you sit there ogling me?' she asked, her face colouring.

'I never ogle,' he drawled. 'I admire. Like an art-lover appreciating a Reubens. Would you like me to undress you?'

'No, I wouldn't! Just you sit where you are,' she ordered reprovingly. She opened the box. The dress was folded neatly between layers of tissue paper and as she withdrew it she felt a thrill of excitement. In a delicate shade of pale green, it flowed and shimmered with a life of its own as only pure silk could. Holding it up at arm's length, she exclaimed, 'It's fabulous! It's simply gorgeous!' Then she gulped. 'But it . . . it's strapless. I've never worn anything like this before.'

'You don't need straps to keep a dress up,' he pointed out with a grin. 'You already have the equipment.'

Reverently she laid the dress over the back of a chair then, turning her back on him, she stripped down to her bra and briefs. Remembering at the last minute, she hurriedly undid her bra and cast it aside. Stepping into the dress, she pulled it up, reached awkwardly behind for the zip, then adjusted the top. Only when she was satisfied that she wouldn't pop out and that the laws of decency would be preserved did she dare to turn and face him for inspection.

He sat at the desk, his blue eyes contemplating her in a silence which stretched and tautened her nerves. The expression on his drawn face was unreadable and she was finally prompted to ask in dejection, 'What's wrong? Don't you like it? Don't just sit there looking at me. At least say something.'

At last she got a reaction. There was a flicker of a smile in his eyes and he spread his hands. 'There are times when words are inadequate. This is one of them.'

A smile of relief lit up her face. 'Then you do like it?'

'Yes, Avalon. I do like it.' He finished his drink, then got to his feet. 'It's perfect for you. But there's something missing.' Retrieving the box she'd put aside in her haste, he removed some more of the tissue paper and uncovered a sash in dark blue and green tartan. 'This goes over your shoulder diagonally, then gets tied at the waist. You'll need a brooch. We'll get that in Inverness.' When he'd arranged the sash to his satisfaction he held her at arm's length to admire the effect, then slowly he drew her closer.

Her heart quickened as his dark features hovered over hers, their lips were almost touching, and she whispered, 'I...I'll have to have something done about my hair. It's a mess. I could get it cut and——'

A growl of warning came from his throat. 'Don't you dare. I like you the way you are.' To prove the point his fingers entwined themselves in the hair at the back of her head, feeling its cloudy softness, then dropped to her invitingly bare shoulders. His mouth nibbled at her top lip for a moment, tasting and teasing, then his breath felt warm and moist in her ear. 'Adorable little sea-creatures like you only need a comb and brush.'

She trembled in his arms as his lips played sweet havoc with the delicate, sensitive skin of her neck and shoulders and, as his fingers played with the zip at the back of her dress, she moulded her body closer to his, driven by an achingly urgent desire that was heightened by his own obvious arousal.

Another growl came from his throat, this time one of frustration, and he released her reluctantly. In his eyes she saw his battle to control his own rampant desire and she seized the initiative. 'You've got work to do,' she said firmly. 'And I'm interrupting. I think it would be better if I left you now, to get on with it.'

For a moment it looked as if business before pleasure was the last thing on his mind, then he finally conquered the hunger in his eyes and sighed. 'Aye. You're right. I'd better finish that damned report and get it sent off. Run along and see if Mrs MacKay likes the way you look. Her advice on these matters is better than mine.'

By the time she'd gathered up her discarded clothing he was already back at his desk, writing in furious frustration, and he merely grunted when she took her leave.

As she closed the library door behind her she paused, and rested for a moment to allow her fluttering heartbeat to return to normal and the flush of sexual excitement to leave her face, then she thoughtfully made her way towards the kitchen. Only a matter of days ago she'd been adamantly determined that the only way Fraser would get her to attend the Grand Ceilidh was if he dragged her by the scruff of the neck but now, because of this dress, she was as excited at the prospect as a child looking forward to Christmas. And, with the tingle of Fraser's kisses still lingering on her lips and skin, it was easy enough to convince herself that he had fallen in love with her at last. Her head was well and truly in the clouds but in reality nothing had really changed, and she had an uneasy premonition that she was going to trip up and fall flat on her face.

Mrs MacKay was as enthusiastic and full of praise for the dress as Fraser had been. Especially for the colour. Putting her head to one side, she studied the dress for a moment, then nodded in satisfaction. 'It'll go well with the necklace, Avalon. You'll be the belle of the ball and no mistake.'

She gave the housekeeper a puzzled look. 'What necklace?'

'The Suilvach emerald necklace,' Mrs MacKay said innocently. 'Didn't Fraser show it to you?'

Avalon shrugged. 'No. He mentioned a brooch for the sash but nothing about a necklace.'

'Well, it's a large emerald surrounded by diamonds, actually,' the housekeeper went on chattily. 'It's been in the family for generations. There's a tradition that at a Clan gathering the Chief always places it around the neck of the woman he wants to marry. I dare say he'll be waiting until the Grand Ceilidh before he puts it round yours.' She paused thoughtfully. 'Mind you, I'm surprised he didn't even show it to you. He keeps it in the safe in the library.'

'He probably forgot,' Avalon said in a subdued voice. 'He's very tired.'

'Aye. That must be it.'

There was, of course, another reason why he hadn't shown it to her, Avalon told herself bleakly. He was keeping it for someone else. Someone called Pamela.

An hour later, dressed in jeans and anorak, she came downstairs on her way out, then paused at the library door before glancing cautiously inside. Fraser was face down on the couch, fast asleep. Tiptoeing in, she stood gazing down at him in silence, her thoughts and emotions a turbulent mixture of tenderness and vexation. Fetching a travelling-rug from the back of a chair, she spread it over him gently, careful not to waken him, then she left, closing the door quietly behind her.

Disconsolately she made her way round the bay towards the village. She wished that Mrs MacKay had never told her about the necklace. Then she wouldn't be thinking now of Pamela. She hadn't once mentioned her name since she'd made that promise to Fraser after the argument in the hotel bar. Even afterwards—when she'd gone up to the cottage and apologised to Kirsty for her rudeness and Kirsty had brought up Pamela's name while they were having tea—even then she'd held up her hand and smiled. 'No, Kirsty. I don't want to hear anything about Pamela. I'm not interested in her.'

Kirsty had nodded happily. 'Good! That's as it should be.'

But now, with the Grand Ceilidh drawing nearer, it was getting harder and harder to keep these thoughts of Pamela at bay. She'd never even met the girl but that didn't stop her imagination from running riot.

Pamela would be stunningly beautiful and perfectly groomed. Very upper crust with the 'right' kind of background and breeding and no blood-ties to the

Clan. In short, she had every qualification Fraser was looking for in a wife. And no one up here would dare question his choice. He'd even manage to get round Kirsty somehow or other.

The report Fraser had written, plus an acrimonious telephone call with someone from a government department that very evening, resulted in another burst of activity from Fraser. Meetings in Edinburgh and Brussels meant that he was away most of the time, defending the rights of the West Coast fishermen to make a decent living.

When it was all finally settled and he had time to relax there was only a week left until the Grand Ceilidh.

'We're going to Inverness today, Avalon,' he informed her over breakfast. 'Wear something a bit more formal than jeans and a sweater for a change.'

The morning was already warm and sunny and she'd been looking forward to a lazy day just swimming and sunbathing on the beach but, guessing that he'd just gone through enough arguments to last a lifetime, she managed to convey an impression of eagerness. 'Good! It'll be nice to get back to civilisation for a while at least.'

His blue eyes looked at her sharply across the table, then he pushed his empty cup away, stood up and said, 'I'm going to check the car. Be as quick as you can.'

Upstairs she rummaged around in the wardrobe then decided on a pearl-grey two-piece suit in light-weight linen and a dark green blouse.

By the time she was ready Fraser had brought his pride and joy from the garage and was busy checking the oil and tyre pressures. The old Jaguar, its chrome and dark blue paintwork gleaming in the sun, looked impatient to stretch its legs. 'That's an old E-type!' she exclaimed in admiration.

He straightened up with a look of surprise on his face and an unaccustomed twinkle in his eyes. 'What does a pretty young thing like you know about cars?'

She bristled. 'My ex-boss used to have one of those. He thought more of it than he did of his wife.'

He patted the bonnet affectionately. 'Aye. Women or fast cars. Sometimes it's a difficult choice for a man to make.'

'Well, I suppose it all depends on the kind of thrill he's after,' she murmured acidly. She got into the passenger seat, adjusted the seatbelt then sank back into the firmly cushioned leather.

Normally she was the worst kind of car passenger imaginable. She was one of those neurotic freaks whose feet would be working an imaginary clutch and brake pedal in a desperate wish to be in charge of her own fate. With Fraser it was different. He seemed to be a natural extension of the sleek, powerful piece of machinery and she felt completely at ease as he made it tear along the narrow roads and through the twisting glens of the Western Highlands.

After a few miles of doing nothing but admire the rugged grandeur of the scenery his silence began to weigh on her, and she attempted a casual conversation.

'What's Inverness like?'

'Very busy. Very clean. Good hotels, bars, restaurants, cinemas, discos and theatre. All the things you're so obviously missing.'

There'd been an unmistakable tone of reproof in his answer and she frowned at him. 'What makes you think there's anything I've been missing?'

He kept his eyes on the road ahead, not even bothering to answer, and she wondered what it was she'd said to annoy him now. Dammit! Talking to him was like walking on eggs. Was it really worth all the hassle?

She sat for the next few miles, pouting her lips and racking her brains, then she looked at him uneasily. 'Look . . . when I said that it would be nice to get back to civilisation again I wasn't running down Suilvach and calling it uncivilised or anything like that. As a matter of fact I like the place. It . . . it sort of grows on you.'

She looked at his profile closely to see if her words were having any effect on him, but all she got for her pains was a neutral-sounding grunt.

She folded her arms crossly. If he didn't want to believe her, there was no way she could convince him that she really was getting used to living there. She was beginning to know most of the people by sight and a good many by name. Perhaps it was because their lives were ruled by the laws of nature—winds and tides being more important than clocks—that they always had the time to stop for a friendly chat.

She knew the trouble with Fraser, of course. Suilvach might be small and insignificant on the map but it was his dominion and she'd inadvertently ruffled his pride. Any minute he was liable to stop the car and throw her out, she thought dismally.

Finally he was the one to break the chilly silence. 'What do you and young Jamie get to talk about?' he asked. 'I hear that the pair of you have been meeting each evening by the harbour wall then spending half an hour chatting away like fishwives.'

'That's a secret between Jamie and me,' she said stiffly.

He spared her a cynical glance. 'Secret? Aren't you being a bit childish?'

'Not in the least,' she retorted. 'I dare say there are lots of secrets you keep from me.' She paused, then added recklessly, 'Like Pamela, for instance.'

She could almost feel the temperature drop in the car and she winced. Why hadn't she kept her mouth shut? Look what had happened the last time she'd mentioned Pamela. He'd nearly wiped the floor with her.

'I told you that my relationship with Pamela has nothing to do with you,' he said grimly.

'I know what you told me,' she shouted back at him angrily. 'What makes you think I'm the least bit interested in your "relationship" with her? I know she's a friend of yours and I was just curious to know if you'd taken the opportunity to visit her while you were in Edinburgh. I'm only making conversation, after all. Trying to be companionable. That isn't a crime, is it? You don't have to sit there with steam blowing out of your ears.'

His blue eyes flickered over her momentarily before returning to the road and he grunted, 'I did visit her. I spent a couple of nights at her family estate. I always make a point of staying with friends if I'm in their part of the country.'

'Good,' she said hotly. 'That's all you needed to say instead of jumping down my throat.' She counted to ten, then said casually, 'I'd like to meet her some time. I suppose she'll be coming to the Grand Ceilidh?'

She saw the edge of his thin smile as he said quietly, 'Oh, yes, you'll definitely be meeting her. She would never dream of missing this Grand Ceilidh.'

'Good,' she said again. 'Good. I'm glad.' She turned her head away and gazed miserably out of the window, unable to keep up the pretence any longer.

They arrived in Inverness a little after midday. The car park was by the riverside just across from the ancient castle on the hill and after locking the car securely Fraser led her across the bridge towards the town centre.

'We'll have a bar lunch first, then do a bit of shopping,' he decreed. 'Then I've got a surprise for you.' He glanced at his watch. 'In two hours' time, to be precise.'

She wasn't into surprises—not his kind, anyway— but she refrained from saying so in case he went into his moody mode again.

He paused at a busy street corner and questioned her drily, 'What kind of pubs do you prefer—lager and loud pop music or fancy cocktails and fake furniture?'

She put her hands on her hips and gave him a hard look. 'You don't know me at all, do you? You've no idea what kind of person I really am.'

'No, I don't,' he drawled easily, almost amused at her scathing reproach. 'I only know the things you've told me about but little else. We haven't really had enough time together, have we? But I'm trying to learn.'

'Well, the first thing to learn is that I hate loud music and I loathe cocktails, so if you've nothing better to offer let's just skip the pub and go to a decent restaurant instead.'

He offered her his arm with mock gallantry. 'Fair enough. I know the very place.'

The restaurant he took her to offered a good view of the yachts and pleasure-craft negotiating the canal which led south into Loch Ness. Not feeling particularly hungry, she settled for a light omelette and coffee while he attacked a gigantic T-bone steak like a hungry wolf.

When he'd paid the bill they strolled back towards the town centre, which seemed to be drowning under a sea of tourists, and she clung to his arm as he carved his way along the crowded pavements. Finally he turned into the relative tranquillity of a very up-market shopping mall. Unlike the main streets with their supermarkets and chain-stores, the shops here were small, select and very expensive.

He made his way to one particular shop which specialised in Highland dress and accessories and the middle-aged woman behind the counter greeted him like an old friend. They conversed for a few moments in Gaelic then Fraser introduced her. 'Mairi, this is Miss Avalon Rivers. She requires a brooch for a sash.'

The woman gave her a friendly smile. 'I think I have the very thing for you, Avalon.' Sliding open a glass display cabinet she extracted a brooch on a black velvet pad and laid it on the counter proudly. 'Freshwater pearls from the Tay, mounted on polished silver. That's the only one in the country. Only ten were made and nine of them went to one of our customers in the Middle East.'

Avalon gazed at it in fascination, too afraid even to touch it.

Fraser was watching her expression. 'Well? Do you like it?'

She nodded and swallowed. 'It . . . it's beautiful.'

'Right, Mairi. Wrap it up.'

He hadn't even asked the price, she thought weakly.

'She'll also need something for her hair,' he said thoughtfully. 'Something to tie it back with. Can you manage that?'

'Aye. No problem. We have clasps, but nothing that would look right in that bonny blonde hair.' She reached up to a shelf and found a spool of bright red tartan ribbon. She cut off a length then, coming from behind the counter, she gathered Avalon's long tresses together at the back and tied the ribbon in a bow.

Fraser studied the result, then nodded in satisfaction. 'That'll do.'

Avalon stood by his side but averted her eyes as he wrote out a cheque. For her peace of mind she had no wish to know how much he'd just spent. Anger and gratitude didn't mix.

They left the mall and this time he took her into one of the more popular chain-stores. He studied the display of the floor plan then they took the escalator up to the ladies' millinery department.

'What are we doing here?' she asked, looking around mystified.

'I'm buying you a hat.'

'I don't wear hats. I never wear hats. I don't suit them.'

He ignored her protest and signalled to an assistant. 'Madam here would like a hat. Something with a wide brim. The wider the better.'

The assistant smiled at her. 'Any particular colour, madam?'

Avalon looked at her helplessly, then shrugged. 'Something to go with this suit, I suppose.'

As soon as the assistant was out of earshot she whirled on Fraser and hissed irritably, 'Will you please tell me what you're playing at? You told me that you liked my hair the way it was and now you've got it tied back with a ribbon and you're insisting that I wear a damned hat!'

'I have a reason,' he snapped. 'Just do as you're told and stop arguing. You promised to trust me, didn't you?'

She sighed again and gave up in defeat, and ten minutes later she was back out on the street wearing a light grey hat with an enormous floppy brim. 'You'd better have a good reason for making me wear this,' she muttered at him rebelliously. 'I told you that I don't suit hats.'

'You look positively charming,' he assured her drily.

'Positively idiotic, you mean,' she retorted.

They'd only gone another few yards when he stopped once more to gaze in a window and before she could protest she was dragged into another shop.

'Ladies' sunglasses,' he told the shopkeeper. 'The largest pair you've got.'

Avalon folded her arms, tapped her foot, and gazed at the ceiling.

Two minutes later she was out on the street again with her eyes hidden behind Polaroids the size of small saucers and the brim of that ridiculous hat flapping in her face. She wondered bleakly what was going to happen next. Green wellington boots?

He glanced at his watch. 'We've half an hour to kill. What would you like to do...have another coffee?'

'I'd like to hide in a dark alley somewhere but I don't suppose you'd let me,' she retorted. 'I guess I'll have to settle for another coffee. Try to find some place where there aren't any other customers, will you?'

'If I do, you can bet the coffee won't be worth drinking,' he grunted.

'I'm willing to take the risk.'

They found a quiet little backstreet café and when they'd been served she removed her sunglasses, blinked, then eyed him quizzically. 'I don't suppose you'd care to tell me what this is all about, would you? I mean...take this hat. It's ridiculous! Even you must see that. You...you're not trying to make a fool of me, are you?'

She could have sworn that for the briefest instant his blue eyes held a hint of sympathy, then it vanished and he dismissed her accusation brusquely. 'Of course not. Very shortly you'll be glad that you're wearing that hat and those glasses. After our business is finished in this town you can throw the damn things in the river for all I care.'

She took a long, hard look across the table at those dark and potently masculine features and she suddenly experienced the blind, trusting faith of a child and knew that if he told her to crawl over broken glass she'd get down on her knees without a murmur.

When it was time to leave he led her outside, hailed a taxi, and quietly muttered the destination in the driver's ear.

Five minutes later they were deposited outside an imposing-looking building and she looked at Fraser in bewilderment. 'You're taking me to court?'

He had a firm grip of her arm. 'Aye. It's only the Sheriff Court. County Court to you. But there's a High Court judge sitting today. 'We're merely spectators. Now put those glasses back on.'

She had one blinding light of revelation and she gasped, 'Smith! It's Smith and his gang, isn't it?' She tried to wriggle out of his grasp. 'I'm not going in there. They . . . they'll recognise me.'

He took her hand in his and gave it a reassuring squeeze. 'I doubt it very much. Not in that disguise.'

CHAPTER EIGHT

'THANK God that's over,' Avalon said with heartfelt relief. 'Why didn't you tell me? You kept it a secret until I was actually in the building.'

'Would you have come otherwise?' he asked drily. 'I don't think so.'

She recalled how she'd tried to wrench herself free from his grip. If he'd given her half a chance she'd have taken to her heels. 'You're right,' she admitted ruefully. 'But I warn you now, Fraser. Don't ever spring any more surprises like that on me. My heart won't stand it.'

It was early evening and there were only a few other people scattered around the hotel lounge bar. 'At least I can get rid of this stupid hat now,' she muttered.

'You can get rid of the glasses as well if you want. But keep the ribbon in your hair. It suits you.' He grinned, then raised his glass. 'Here's to justice.'

She sipped her own drink, feeling calm and with a glow of self-satisfaction. Smith had put her through hell and when they'd led him and his cohorts into the dock all the memories had flooded back. She'd almost drowned because of him. There had been a real moment of fear when he'd gazed around the courtroom, but his eyes had slid over her without recognition.

She laid her glass down and snorted. 'Bloody drug smugglers. Did you see the look on their faces when the judge gave them ten years each?'

'It would have been more if they hadn't taken their lawyer's advice to plead guilty.' He eyed her in speculative silence, then said quietly, 'I suppose you realise that this puts our relationship on a new footing?'

Wondering what he was getting at, she gave him a slightly puzzled smile. 'Does it? In what way?'

He shrugged his wide shoulders. 'Smith can't implicate you out of spite now. The trial is over and there was no mention of your presence on the boat. So now the danger is past and you're free to go.'

Her inner glow of satisfaction dimmed and went out altogether. 'Free to go? Go where?' Her voice wavered in a sort of disbelief.

'Wherever you want.' His mouth turned down in regret then he explained further. 'The threat of Smith was a lever I used to keep you at Suilvach. I don't have that lever any more. I've no right to keep you against your will. If you want to return to London there's nothing I can do to stop you.' He paused and his eyes searched her face, waiting for a response.

The unexpectedness of it numbed her mind for a moment. Her mouth felt full of ashes and she didn't dare trust her voice. Finally she swallowed. 'Do...do you want me to go?'

He made no reply and his face was cold and unemotional, like something carved from dark, weathered stone.

Of course he wanted her to go, she told herself bitterly. It was all too achingly clear to her, now, how big a fool she was. She'd just been a toy to pass the time with and now that he'd had his fun with her he wanted rid of her embarrassing presence before Pamela, his girlfriend, arrived on the scene.

That had to be the answer.

And yet...?

She could be wrong. She could be in danger of making an even bigger fool of herself by misreading his motives and intentions. After all, she knew just how ruthless he could be when it came to getting his own way. If he really did want her out of his life, all he needed to do was drive off into the sunset, leaving her here with a train ticket south and a severe case of heartbreak.

Somehow she managed to give a casual shrug as if the whole business wasn't really important enough to worry about. 'I think it would be rude if I left without saying goodbye to Jamie...and Kirsty...and Aileen...and all the others I've got to know. And, if it's all the same to you, I was really looking forward to the Grand Ceilidh. I've heard so much about it.'

His eyes regarded her shrewdly as he considered her reply, then he gave a thin, sardonic smile. 'Aye. Just like a woman. Can't resist the opportunity to wear a glamorous dress.'

Her nails dug into her palms and she felt like screaming at him—No, you stupid man! Can't you see that I'm in love with you? I want to stay because there's a chance in a million that you'll fall in love with me. I want to stay because I want to be your wife. Instead, she managed a self-deprecating smile. 'Yes. You're right. Just like a woman. That's me.'

In some subtle way his harsh features softened and he nodded. 'I'm glad. In fact I'd have been very disappointed if you'd decided to leave.'

Her heart lifted a little. 'You would?'

There was a definite smile on his face now. 'Yes. Extremely disappointed. You'd have spoilt my plans for the rest of the night.'

'Oh? What plans are you talking about?' Was that a calculating smile on his face or was it the real thing? She couldn't make up her mind.

'As soon as I knew the date of the trial I phoned for a booking in this hotel,' he told her blandly. 'I guessed that neither of us would feel like the long drive home in the evening. There's a suite upstairs ready and waiting for us.'

'I see...' Her pulse was beginning to quicken again. 'That was very thoughtful of you.'

'Yes...' he drawled with dry amusement. 'Wasn't it?' He signalled the waiter for another round of drinks and gave her that predatory grin again. 'I've a feeling that this is going to be a night to remember, Avalon.'

Somewhere in the night a clock chimed three and she was still awake. In the bed beside her Fraser was stretched out on his back fast asleep, his chest rising and falling to the regular rhythm of his breathing. Careful not to waken him, she snuggled herself closer, welding her own warm flesh to his. The fingers of her left hand traced a gentle exploration of his body, feeling the smooth skin and hard muscles of his torso, and she tasted the slight saltiness of him with her lips and tongue.

If there were to be any regrets they could wait for the dawn, but at the moment she was too satiated and beguiled to care about anything. Anyway, she'd surrendered to his demand to spend the night with him readily enough. Not because she was afraid that a refusal would turn him against her completely—her own moral integrity would never have allowed her to jeopardise her self-respect in that way. She wasn't for sale in any way whatsoever. The simple truth was that she was a more than willing victim to her own weakness for him. When those blue eyes of his flashed at her with their promise of sensual delights her body seemed to dissolve and her brain ceased to function. Even the mere thought of being in his arms once more was enough to sap her energy and leave her as defenceless as a kitten confronting the tiger of her own aching need.

Their lovemaking had begun with a provocatively languorous appreciation of each other's bodies. Hands and lips had caressed, fondled and kissed as they'd shared in each other's pleasure, both of them giving and receiving with equal abandonment. What she had was his and all of him belonged to her with no thought of holding anything back. She was his willing pupil and he was the master craftsman who moulded and shaped her responses and taught her things her wildest dreams had never imagined.

Her body seemed to ripen and blossom and, like a flower, she opened under the hot sun of his passion. Then she was filled with him and she quivered and moaned as he moved in long, slow thrusts which drove him ever deeper and deeper. At last, when the sweet ecstasy became almost too much to bear, she heard a groan rumble from his throat. The dam holding back the hot tide of his passion burst and they came together in a frenzied, gasping, clutching climax.

Afterwards they lay passively in each other's arms for a while, then he dragged her out of bed. They'd showered together, soaping each other and cavorting under the hot water like a couple of kids, then they'd sat, curled up on the rug in front of the fire, sipping iced champagne.

When the bottle was finally finished he'd got to his feet and stood towering over her, the firelight flickering over his perfect physique. Her gaze had travelled over him — the wide shoulders, deep chest, slim waist and hips, the thick, powerful thighs. She'd tried but failed to suppress a giggle. 'By the look of you you're ready to do it all over again.'

He had glanced down at himself and grinned. 'Aye. It must be the oysters we had for dinner.' Bending down, he had scooped her effortlessly into his arms and carried her back to the bed.

In the morning he shook her gently awake and she blinked in the sunlight streaming through the window. Squeezing her eyes shut again she cautiously opened one and looked up from the pillow. He was fresh and clean shaved and wearing a short, loosely tied bathrobe.

'What time is it?' she muttered drowsily.

'Nine o'clock. I've had your breakfast sent up.'

She groaned. 'I didn't fall asleep till five. Just let me lie another hour.'

'You'll feel better after your coffee. Now, sit up and take this tray.'

'I can't sit up. I've no clothes on,' she said plaintively.

He chuckled. 'I know. I took them off you last night, remember?'

She sighed. 'Well, don't just stand there looking at me. Be a gentleman and get me something to wear.'

Laying the breakfast tray at the foot of the bed, he fetched his shirt and tossed it at her.

'Thanks.' She examined the tray and smiled up at him. 'Cornflakes. Toast and honey. Two boiled eggs. You're spoiling me. What are you having?'

His blue eyes gleamed and he threatened her with a make-believe growl. 'I'll be jumping in there and having you for breakfast if you don't hurry and cover yourself up.' He waited till she'd buttoned the front of the shirt then he said casually, 'I had mine sent up an hour ago, along with the morning papers. There's a report of yesterday's trial and verdict if you're interested.'

For a moment the nightmare memories returned and she shivered. 'No. That part of my life is finished. I just want to forget all about it.'

He gave an understanding nod and changed the subject. 'Business at Suilvach can take care of itself for the next few days. I feel like a break. We could stay here or drive south. Visit Edinburgh, perhaps? I'll leave the choice to you.'

'That sounds good,' she said enthusiastically, then added quickly, 'Not Edinburgh, though.'

He gave a dark, puzzled frown. 'What have you got against Edinburgh?'

Well, Pamela lived there, didn't she? He might just get it into his head to pay her another visit. 'Not a thing,' she dissembled. 'I've heard it's very beautiful but the place I've always wanted to see is Gretna Green. You know... the place where all the young runaway couples go to get married over the anvil in the blacksmith's shop.' She smiled at him innocently. 'It sounds very romantic.' She took a spoonful of cornflakes, munched them, then added, 'I'd like to see the Loch Ness monster as well.'

He laughed at her apparent childishness. 'I can show you Loch Ness, but as for the monster...'

She pouted her lips in disappointment. 'You mean there isn't really a monster at all?'

'I never said that...' He was looking at her suspiciously now. 'There might be or there might not be.'

She spooned another helping of cornflakes into her mouth, chewed it reflectively, then gave a determined nod. 'There must be. If this is the land of Fire Magic and fairies there's no reason why there shouldn't be monsters.'

He aimed a rolled-up sock at her but she ducked in time.

She saw Loch Ness. All twenty-odd miles of it. But no monster. Plenty of tourists, though. Every lay-by and car park was crowded with them, all aiming their cameras hopefully at the mysterious stretch of dark water. Then further south, through Fort William, packed with more tourists.

The sun beat down from a blue, cloudless sky but did nothing to dispel the chill as the Jaguar flitted through the shadows and past the ghosts of eerie Glencoe. Then up on to the bleak desolation of Rannoch Moor and the flanks of the Black Mount and down into the softly colourful beauty of Loch Lomond-side and then the northern commuter suburbs of Glasgow.

They spent a couple of hours shopping for a change of clothes in the city, then resumed their journey south into the hills and forests of the wild Border country. Late in the afternoon they left the beaten track and booked into an attractive little country hotel.

After dinner that evening they strolled by the river, returning just as darkness fell to the warmth and hospitality of the hotel bar for a nightcap.

That night, in a huge four-poster bed, they made love again ... and again ...

The following day they headed for Gretna, the small village nestling just this side of the border, and at the famous anvil they found themselves being asked to stand in as witnesses by a young French couple who were about to be wed. She and Fraser were delighted to oblige and in return for the privilege Fraser insisted in treating them to a sumptuous meal in the local hotel.

An hour later they were heading north once more and Fraser suddenly grinned at her from the driving seat. 'Well, that was Gretna. Did it come up to your expectations?'

Avalon had been quietly thoughtful for the last few minutes and she smiled back at him. 'I was impressed by your generosity. Inviting them for a meal. I think they really appreciated that.'

'Aye...well, they were a decent enough pair of youngsters but you could see they were a bit strapped for cash. A Coke and a hamburger is no way to start married life.'

She remembered the look in the French girl's eyes— Colette had been her name—as her handsome partner had held her hand over the anvil. She remembered something else as well—something she wasn't proud of but a feeling that couldn't be denied—a tiny stab of jealousy. Pushing the thought aside she watched the countryside roll by then asked, 'How did it all start? The anvil and everything.'

'The English started it,' Fraser said quietly. 'Young lovers, denied their parents' permission to marry, discovered that if they eloped and fled over the border into Scotland they could be legally married provided they were over the age of sixteen.'

She chewed over that piece of information for a while, then gave her considered opinion. 'If you ask me, sixteen is far too young for a girl to marry.'

He raised an eyebrow at her. 'Don't you think that depends on the girl?'

'No,' she said decisively. 'A girl of sixteen hasn't enough experience of life. She might choose the wrong man and live to regret it.'

He gave her a sideways reproving glance. 'A girl of any age can be mistaken about a man. As they say, love is blind. But up here we've always taken the position that if a girl is old enough to bear and look after a child she should be allowed to marry.'

She sat back and sighed. There was no answer to that.

It was late in the evening, five days later, when they arrived back at Suilvach. Tired though he was after the long drive Fraser retired to the library to catch up on his correspondence, leaving her to the tender mercies of Mrs MacKay in the kitchen. She immediately demanded to know every little detail of her trip with Fraser. Relaxing over a welcome cup of hot coffee Avalon related a highly censored version of all the places they'd been and things they'd done.

Mrs MacKay, who could read between the lines as well as anyone else, seemed pleased and said enigmatically, 'Well . . . it won't be long now. Kirsty will be pleased that everything is working out well.'

'What won't be long?' she asked, frowning at the housekeeper.

'Why . . . you and Fraser! He'll be putting that necklace round your neck at the Grand Ceilidh. It's tomorrow. You surely hadn't forgotten, had you?'

'Oh... Yes...' She got up hurriedly and went to the range to pour herself another coffee. If only she could feel as convinced about Fraser's intentions as Mrs MacKay seemed to be. The last few days had been like a honeymoon in all but name. There had been lots of passion and sex but very little romance. She'd given herself gladly to Fraser but never once, not even at the very heights of their passion, had he murmured in her ear that he loved her. He'd been generous to a fault and considerate, and he seemed to enjoy her company and conversation, but that was as far as it had gone. Perhaps that was as far as he intended it to go.

She turned from the range and smiled at the house-keeper. 'I imagine you'll be very busy getting everything ready for the big event. I'll give you a hand tomorrow.' The busier she kept herself the less time she'd have to think.

Mrs MacKay thanked her for the offer but turned it down gracefully, 'It's all organised. There are a couple of girls from the village coming in the morning to do the heavy work. Besides, Fraser won't be too pleased if he sees you running around in jeans and sweater. He'll be expecting you to look your prettiest when the guests start arriving.'

It was ten-thirty when Avalon knocked gently on the library door and let herself in. 'I'm sorry if I disturbed you, Fraser. I'm going upstairs to bed. I...I just wanted to say goodnight.'

He laid his pen aside and gestured at the chair opposite. 'Sit down, Avalon. I want a few words with you before you go up.' He waited till she'd sat down then he reached for the decanter and poured a couple of drinks. 'Take this.'

'Thanks.' She wondered what was on his mind.

He sipped his own drink, then regarded her gravely. 'We're all going to have a busy day tomorrow, Avalon. I want things to go as smoothly as possible. I don't want any trouble. I'm expecting you to act with dignity.'

She frowned at him. 'Act with dignity? I'm not sure I know what you're getting at.'

His blue eyes were as sharp and cynical as the thin smile on his lips. 'I think you know exactly what I'm getting at. Pamela will be here.'

Her knuckles grew white around the glass. 'Yes. I know.' She tried to keep her voice as unemotional as possible despite the chill of disappointment stabbing her heart. 'Are you suggesting that there will be trouble between me and Pamela?' she asked calmly.

'It's a possibility,' he pointed out drily. 'Women are jealous creatures by nature. Things might be said. Tempers ruffled.'

She laid her drink firmly on the desk and got up. 'If you're afraid that I'll tell your girlfriend that you and I have just spent the last few nights sleeping with each other you needn't worry.' Her voice wasn't calm now. It was shaking. 'I've still got some pride and self-respect left.' She paused and eyed him bitterly. 'I think it would be better for all concerned if I left first thing in the morning. Then you'd have nothing to worry about.'

'I gave you your chance to leave right after the trial,' he said quietly. 'You didn't take it and now the offer is closed. You said that you'd attend the Ceilidh and I expect you to be there.'

It didn't make any sense to her and she looked at him helplessly. 'But why? Surely it would be less embarrassing for you if I weren't there.'

'I have my reasons.' His features were hard and uncompromising. 'I asked you once to trust me. You gave me your promise. Are your promises so easily broken?'

'No...' she wavered. 'But I——'

He cut her off abruptly. 'That's all I've got to say on the subject, Avalon.'

For a moment she stood glaring at him, angered at his curt dismissal, then she snapped, 'I only came in here to say goodnight. Now I wish I hadn't bothered.' Stiffly she turned and marched out of the room.

It was impossible to sleep and she lay in her bed staring up at the darkened ceiling, her mind in a turmoil. She should have taken the opportunity to leave when he'd offered it, but she'd been conceited enough to think that she could steal his love from another woman. Well, she'd failed—but that was her fault, not his. He was looking for something more than sexual attraction and physical pleasure—some mysterious quality that she was lacking but Pamela obviously had.

That could be why he was being so insistent about her attending the Ceilidh. All the important members of the Clan from here and abroad would be there along with the local gentry and aristocracy. She was bound to do or say something stupid. But Pamela wouldn't. She'd know how to conduct herself at these affairs. Perhaps that was his reason! Hoping that she'd make a fool of herself in front of everyone thereby proving that she wasn't fit to be the First Lady of the Clan.

The questions were still torturing her mind when she heard the roar of a car engine in the distance. It wasn't the same throaty growl of the Jaguar. This was harsher and higher pitched. Lights reflected on the window and lit up the room briefly as the noise grew louder and closer. Finally she heard the screech of tyres on gravel, then the impatient blare of a horn.

Getting out of bed she walked over to the window and, by squinting sideways, had a good view of the broad steps leading up from the drive to the doorway. The front door opened, allowing light to spill out, and she saw Fraser emerge and descend to meet the visitor. The driver got out of the car—a tall, slim and elegant girl with dark hair. When she threw her arms around Fraser's neck and kissed him passionately on the mouth Avalon turned from the window and drew a deep, painful breath. She had a good idea who Fraser would be sleeping with tonight.

Avalon had her usual jog in the morning and arrived back to find the kitchen empty although there was a pot of coffee ready. She poured herself a cup, then went in search of the housekeeper and found her in the ballroom supervising the two local girls who'd come along to help. They were setting up long tables on one side of the room, presumably for the cold buffet.

Mrs MacKay smiled at her. 'I'll be with you in a moment, Avalon.'

'Don't worry about me,' she said quietly. 'I can make my own breakfast. I just wondered where you'd got to. Are you quite sure there's nothing I can do to help?' She had to find some way of keeping her mind occupied today or she'd crack up.

The note of quiet desperation in her voice wasn't lost on Mrs MacKay, who looked at her keenly. 'That's very kind of you, Avalon. I dare say that another pair of hands would be useful. Anyway, Fraser is away at the moment. He left five minutes ago for Inverness Airport to meet some people off the plane.'

Well, that was one piece of good news at least. The less she saw of Fraser today, the better.

Mrs MacKay gave the two girls some more instructions, then left them to it and led the way back to the kitchen. 'One of the guests arrived late last night. I had to start cooking a meal at midnight.'

'Yes . . .' murmured Avalon. 'That was Pamela, wasn't it? I heard her car.' She paused, then said innocently, 'She's quite a frequent visitor here, isn't she?'

'Aye. She is that.'

'You sound as if you don't like her very much.'

'Do I?'

From the abruptness of the reply followed by tightly pressed lips Avalon knew she'd made a mistake. It had surely been the height of bad manners to put Mrs MacKay on the spot like that and ask her to pass comment on one of her employer's guests.

'Look . . . I'm sorry,' she said hastily.

Mrs MacKay eyed her warily for a moment and then smiled. 'Ach . . . it doesn't matter. Now, just you sit down at the table while I make you a bit of breakfast.'

Avalon didn't argue. The housekeeper was edgy enough without her making things worse. She was feeling tired and frayed at the seams herself, come to that. Well into the small hours of the morning she'd tossed and turned in her bed, agonising over the thought of Fraser and Pamela together.

Damn Pamela! Damn Fraser! And most of all damn herself for ever falling in love with such a man. Surely if she'd tried just a little bit harder she could have resisted the lure of those magnetic blue eyes—she could have fought harder against the aching desire to be crushed in those arms...to feel that hard, demanding mouth against hers...to have her own soft flesh dominated by his virile masculinity...

Yes. She could have resisted. But she'd been weak and she'd yielded willingly. Now there was a price to pay...

There was a good chance that she was pregnant but the idea of remaining here until she knew for certain was out of the question. Tomorrow morning, come hell or high water, she was returning to London. If it did transpire that she was carrying Fraser's child it would be her secret. He would never hear from her again. She'd just join the ranks of countless other single women who were able to be loving, caring mothers as well as holding down a job.

She'd just finished her breakfast and was doing the washing-up when she heard Mrs MacKay make a sound of annoyance and reach hurriedly for the coffee-pot. 'It's for Pamela,' she explained testily. 'I was to waken her with coffee at nine-thirty. It's already gone that.'

Avalon glanced up at the wall clock. 'Only five minutes.'

'Aye. Well, she's a great one for punctuality. If she says nine-thirty she means it.'

While the coffee was brewing Mrs MacKay busied herself preparing a silver tray with cup and saucer, fresh cream in a jug and a sugar bowl.

Avalon's eyes grew thoughtful. She was beginning to understand now why Pamela had got the nickname of 'lady'. Well, even 'ladies' never looked their best first thing in the morning and she had a sudden urge to see just what Pamela had to offer under her smart hairstyle, make-up and expensive clothes.

When the coffee jug had been filled and placed on the tray she said, 'I'll take it up to her.'

Mrs MacKay looked doubtful. 'Well...I'm not sure if...'

She gave a pleading smile. 'I'm sure Fraser would like me to welcome the guests. I can apologise to her for not being on hand when she arrived last night.'

The mild piece of deception worked and Mrs MacKay, turning a blind eye to established protocol for the first time in her life, gave in. 'Well... if you put it like that. I can't see how Fraser can object.' She handed over the tray with the merest hint of relief in her eyes. 'She's in the west wing. Her room is on the top floor, second on the left.'

Avalon stared at her in surprise. 'The west wing? Are you sure?'

It was the housekeeper's turn to look surprised. 'Of course I'm sure. I took her there myself last night.'

'Oh...' She closed her mouth abruptly, realising how foolish she must have looked standing there with it hanging open.

'Are you feeling all right?' Mrs MacKay asked solicitously.

'Yes. Of course.' She smiled brightly. 'Second on the left, you said?'

As she made her way upstairs with the tray she wondered if this was such a good idea after all. The discovery that Pamela hadn't been sharing Fraser's room last night simply added to her feeling of confusion. It had been her own fevered imagination which had kept her awake most of the night. An imagination fuelled by jealousy. And perhaps it was jealousy rather than curiosity that was driving her now. Was some dark, destructive part of her subconscious mind demanding a head to head confrontation with her rival?

At the top of the stairs she hesitated, then took a deep breath and made her way along the corridor. She'd simply deliver the coffee, keep her mouth shut and get out as fast as she could.

CHAPTER NINE

THERE was a word for it. Style. Class. Whatever you called it, the woman sitting up in bed had it in plenty. No one had any right to look the way she did first thing in the morning. Fresh make-up. Not one single lock of dark, glossy auburn hair out of place. Even the silk bed-jacket looked as if it had just been delivered from Harrods.

Avalon felt herself flushing under the hard scrutiny of pale grey eyes and she wished she'd thought of changing out of her shapeless jogging-suit.

'Who are you?' Pamela demanded.

'I've brought you your coffee,' Avalon replied stiffly.

Pamela sighed in irritation. 'Yes. I can see that. That isn't what I asked. Where's Mrs MacKay? This coffee should have been here ten minutes ago. I realise that you people up here have no sense of time but there's no excuse for laziness.'

Avalon felt her hackles rise but she clung to her temper by her fingertips and said calmly, 'Mrs MacKay has her hands full at the moment, getting everything ready for the Ceilidh tonight.'

Pamela treated the excuse with a disdainful look and Avalon ignored it, laid the tray on the bedside table and had just turned to make her exit when Pamela's voice brought her up short.

'Run my bath before you leave.'

She stopped and turned, her green eyes dangerously bright. 'You'll have to do that yourself, I'm afraid. I don't work here.'

A delicate eyebrow rose in the air. 'I see ... But since it was you who fetched the coffee I naturally assumed ...' She shrugged indifferently.

'I'm a guest, just like you,' Avalon said in a tightly controlled voice.

The grey eyes regarded her with mild curiosity. 'Then perhaps we'd better introduce ourselves. I'm Pamela Russell. Fraser's fiancée.'

There! Now at last it was out in the open. Not friend ... or acquaintance. Fiancée! Of course she'd known it all along but to hear the actual words spoken... It was like a knife being twisted in her heart.

She answered the look of cold interrogation woodenly. 'I'm Avalon Rivers.'

'Rivers ... ?' Pamela repeated the name a few times then shook her head. 'I'm sorry. It doesn't ring any bells. Should I know you? Have you any connection with the Clan?'

Discretion was telling Avalon that it was time to leave and yet there was something so infuriatingly smug and bitchy about this creature that she felt compelled to stand her ground and give as good as she got. 'None whatsoever,' she answered in a dry voice.

'Then who invited you?'

'Fraser.' She paused, then added, 'It was more of a command than an invitation.'

'Really?' The grey eyes measured Avalon carefully. 'And how long have you known Fraser?'

Avalon kept her voice deliberately light and casual. 'About a month. Ever since I arrived here. Actually, I didn't want to stay but he was quite insistent. He said he wanted to get to know me better.' She went to the door, then stopped and looked back. 'You'd better drink your coffee before it gets cold.'

With a feeling of grim satisfaction she made her way downstairs. Fraser had warned her to act with dignity and not to say anything that might cause trouble. Well, she had acted with dignity, and every word she'd spoken had been the truth. 'Lady' Pamela was welcome to make of it what she wanted. Personally, she didn't give a damn.

She spent the rest of the morning by herself, walking dejectedly along the beach.

What could Fraser possibly see in a woman like that? she asked herself. Granted, Pamela was attractive. Even beautiful might not be too strong a word. But as for personality! It grated on your nerves like a nail on glass. If Fraser was going to spend the rest of his life with her then she genuinely pitied him. The poor fool didn't know what he was letting himself in for.

Of course it could be that he only ever got to see the one side of her. She could be all sweetness and light when she was in his company and only reveal her darker side to people she considered inferior. Still ... Fraser wasn't stupid. If he'd known her for any length of time you'd think he'd have seen through her by now.

When she returned to the house she had a light lunch in the kitchen with Mrs MacKay, who was looking decidedly upset about something. Under Avalon's gentle prodding she explained, 'It's the two girls from the village. They were threatening to walk out unless Pamela left them to get on with their work. She was bothering them.'

'Bothering them?' Avalon queried with a frown. 'In what way?'

'Asking questions about you, mostly. And being very persistent about it. Anyway, I had a word in her ear and she's driven off to the village. I dare say she'll be asking questions there as well.'

Avalon shrugged. 'All she needs to do is to ask me instead of going behind my back. As far as I'm concerned I've got nothing to hide nor have I done anything to be ashamed of.' That was true, but deep inside her she wished she felt as certain as she sounded. There was one thing she had done for sure, and that was to throw the cat among the pigeons. Someone in the village was bound to tell Pamela about the '*caileagh bhan*' who'd been brought by the fairies to marry their Chief. God alone knew what would happen then.

After lunch she helped the girls to carry the large salvers of cold cuts through to the ballroom. The sight took her breath away. The floor gleamed...snow-white linen draped the tables...glassware and crystal sparkled...polished silver dazzled.

She congratulated the two girls on the amount of work they'd put in. 'The room looks beautiful. Will you both be here tonight?'

'Oh, aye,' one of them assured her. 'Everyone gets invited to the Grand Ceilidh.' She smiled a little shyly. 'We're really looking forward to this one. After all, it's special, isn't it?'

Avalon quickly changed the subject, chatted with them for a few more minutes, then retreated upstairs to her room. Slipping off her jogging-suit she had a quick shower then donned a plain skirt and lambs-wool sweater.

When her hair was dry she brushed it vigorously, swearing to herself that she was going to get it cut short as soon as she was away from here. The shorter the better. She might even get it dyed black. It might help to wipe away the memories of Fraser of Suilvach which were sure to haunt her every time she looked in a mirror.

No. That was foolish. It wouldn't do any good. Time would heal the wound but nothing would ever erase the memory of that first night they'd made love in the fireglow—nor the day on the boat when he'd hugged her shivering body close to his to give her warmth. Neither would she ever forget those hypnotic blue eyes... the way he growled at her when he was angry and the way a sudden smile of approval could quicken her heart.

There had been moments of loving tenderness when she was sure that he really did love her but now, as she sat staring at her reflection, she wasn't sure of anything any more. He had her dancing to his whim like a puppet and she had no idea of what he was up to.

The lack of sleep the previous night caught up with her and she lay down on the bed intending to nap for half an hour, but it was five hours later when the gentle shake on her shoulder woke her up.

Mrs MacKay was smiling down at her. 'Here. I've brought you a nice cup of tea.'

She sat up in embarrassment and glanced at the clock. 'My God! Is that the time?'

'It's all right,' the housekeeper said soothingly. 'The Ceilidh won't be starting for another half-hour. I came up earlier but you were out for the count so I decided to leave you. You'll be needing all the rest you can

get before the dancing begins. And don't worry about
not being down to greet the guests. Pamela has already
seen to that.'

Avalon sipped her tea and mentally tried to get her
act together. 'Did Pamela say anything to you when
she got back from the village?' she asked casually.

'No...' Mrs MacKay said thoughtfully. 'But she
seemed awfully angry about something. And I heard
her and Fraser having words about something later
on.' She clucked her tongue as if annoyed at herself
for gossiping about her betters, then she smiled. 'Well,
I'd better get back downstairs.'

Avalon took her tea over to the window and gazed
down into the driveway. Among all the glittering
Daimlers and Mercedeses there were a few battered
pick-ups and family saloons. There was even an old
tractor, and she wondered if that was the one old
Gavin had been driving on the night he'd found her
on the rocks. The idea of going down now and facing
the curious stares of all those people put a knot in
her stomach but reluctantly she went to the bathroom
and splashed cold water on her face.

About fifteen minutes later she was pinning the
pearl and silver brooch to the sash when there was a
gentle knock on the door. Thinking it was Mrs
MacKay again, she called out, 'Come in.'

Pamela entered—tall and elegant, her slim figure
encased in a shimmering red gown and her rich auburn
hair tumbling to her bare shoulders.

Avalon, automatically bracing herself for a torrent
of angry abuse and accusation, was completely taken
aback by the hesitant smile and the quiet, almost
humble tone of Pamela's voice. 'I...I hope you don't
mind me disturbing you, Avalon. I think you and I

should get things sorted out before this goes any further.'

Her green eyes narrowed warily. 'What things?'

Pamela's expression begged forgiveness. 'We got off on the wrong foot this morning, Avalon. It was my fault. All I can do is apologise and say how sorry I am.' She bit her lip, then sighed. 'This is very embarrassing for me...' Her voice dried up and she lowered her eyes.

Avalon began to feel uneasy. An apology? A confession of embarrassment? From Pamela? From her short acquaintance with the woman it seemed completely out of character. But that was the trouble. How well could you really get to know anyone after a short acquaintance? Pamela's distress certainly seemed genuine enough.

'Right now you can't feel any more embarrassed than I do,' she said cautiously, wondering why Pamela had really come to see her.

Pamela gave a vigorous nod. 'I can understand that. He's made love to you, hasn't he?'

She stiffened. 'Did Fraser tell you that?'

'He doesn't have to.' Pamela sighed, then went on bitterly, 'You've been here a month and I know Fraser. If he sees an attractive girl...especially someone as innocent and lovely as you are... God! It makes me sick to think of the way he's taken advantage of you. Not just you...all the others before you arrived on the scene. I've pleaded and argued with him. I've tried time and time again but it never makes any difference. Then, this afternoon...when I found out about you...we had another terrible argument. He's promised to be faithful once we get married...but until then...' She stopped and looked at Avalon helplessly.

That must have been the argument Mrs MacKay had mentioned overhearing, Avalon realised. The knot in her stomach began to get tighter. Doubt crept into her eyes and voice. 'If...if he's as bad as you say then why have you put up with it for so long? I wouldn't.'

'You're right, Avalon,' Pamela said in a low voice of total defeat. 'No woman with an ounce of sense would stand for it. But the world is full of stupid women like me. Love must have been invented by a man. It lets them do anything they like because they know that in the end you'll always forgive them.'

'Then you're a fool,' Avalon retorted hotly. 'Or at least one of us is.'

'Yes. We're both fools, Avalon. Me for believing his promises and you for believing all that nonsense about fairies and Fire Magic.' Her grey eyes regarded Avalon with sympathy. 'Thankfully there are still some decent people in Suilvach who had the good sense to tell me what's been going on. And as for Kirsty...she's well-meaning but just a tiny bit of a charlatan, if you get my meaning. There are people like her all over the Highlands. "Seers", they call themselves. It gives them a certain status and it's easy enough to play on the superstitions that are rife in this part of the country.'

'But what about the fire?' Avalon protested. 'I saw that with my own eyes. It was real.'

'Of course it was real,' Pamela soothed. 'But there's no magic involved. It's quite common up on the moor. Marsh gas. Methane, I think. It just takes a spark to

set it off. As far as I can determine, it was because
of a cigarette-end thrown by Gavin the tractor driver.'

'Are you telling me that everyone knew about it?'
Avalon asked with a feeling of cold betrayal. 'Fraser?
And Kirsty? And ... and Aileen and all the others?'

Pamela gave a delicate shrug. 'The Nevay is a
dangerous place. That's why the village children are
never allowed to play there. They'll tell you it's because of the gas.'

Everything began to drop into place. All her original
fears and doubts about Fraser and Kirsty were proving
to be true. Right from the start the truth had been
staring her in the face but she'd been too blinded by
her own desires to see it.

'There's something else you should know,' Pamela
said in a voice of soft regret.

'No...' Avalon said thickly. 'I...I've heard enough.'

Pamela went on regardless. 'Did he tell you that he
has to be married within two weeks at the latest?'

Her eyes widened. 'No. He didn't.' She clenched
her fists. 'He never even spoke about you. Neither
him nor Kirsty. Whenever I asked he just told me to
mind my own business. And Kirsty just avoided the
question.'

'Well, it's his thirty-fifth birthday soon and if he
isn't married by then he loses the title and it goes to
his uncle,' Pamela explained quietly. 'Fraser won't let
that happen. His uncle is some sort of property
speculator who would sell everything off to the highest
bidder. Fraser and I came to an agreement a long time
ago that when the time was right we'd be married.
And that time is now. He can't put it off any longer.
I'm afraid that his brief affair with you was just the
last fling of his carefree bachelor days.' She paused,

then confessed brokenly, 'I...I'm truly sorry, Avalon.
But I...I had to warn you. You can see that, can't
you?'

'Warn me about what?' she asked in a pain-dulled
voice. 'What else can he do? Hasn't he caused enough
damage already?'

Pamela put an anguished hand to her brow for a
moment, then seemed to gather her courage. 'Have
you thought of the embarrassment, Avalon? It...it
isn't going to be easy for you when you go downstairs. Everyone knows that Fraser has been using you.
But he's their Chief and in their eyes he can do no
wrong. They'll all be laughing at you behind your
back. Well, I want no part of that.'

Avalon's mind was already made up and with a
throat-burning bitterness she undid the brooch and
sash and threw them on the bed. 'Don't worry. He
won't get the chance to humiliate me any more,' she
vowed. 'He and his whole damn Clan can go to hell.
I never want to see him again.'

There was a raw, heavy silence that was finally
broken by a heartfelt sigh from Pamela. 'I don't blame
you, Avalon. I'd feel exactly the same in your position, though I doubt if I'd have the courage to take
it as well as you. Look...I'll make up some excuse.
I'll tell them you've got a headache.'

Avalon stared at her in silence, unable to trust her
voice any more, and when Pamela had retreated from
the room she marched angrily over to the door and
turned the heavy key in the lock.

She caught her reflection in the wardrobe mirror,
face pale and drawn with stress, eyes burning with the
hot flames of resentment. With a shaking hand she
reached round and undid the zip and let the dress fall

to the floor. She grabbed it up, threw it across the back of a chair and donned her jogging-suit.

In the cold grip of despair she threw herself down on the bed and tried to blank out her mind ... to still the painful pounding of her betrayed heart. She heard the music start up in the ballroom below and she pressed her hands to her ears to block out the sound. She squeezed her eyes shut, seeking oblivion in the darkness, but the image of his face was still there, the blue eyes mocking her and the thin, hard lips twisted in a cynical smile.

A sharp knock at the door wrenched her from the pit of despondency and she sat up in bed. The knock came again. More insistent this time. A man's knock. It was him! Getting off the bed she walked to the door and shouted, 'Go away.'

A voice, slightly muffled by the thickness of the door, answered back. 'Avalon? This is Fraser. What's keeping you? Let me in.'

'No!' she yelled back. 'I'm not coming out. I know all about you now. Go away and leave me alone!'

There was a frustrated rattle of the doorknob, then a nerve-stretching silence, and she expected the door to come crashing inwards off its hinges at any moment. When nothing happened she cautiously pressed her ear to one of the panels and heard his footsteps fading into the distance. When she was sure that he had finally gone she wandered disconsolately over to the window and stared, misty-eyed, across the bay towards the village. She was going to miss this place—the peace, the stunning scenery, the friendly people. She could have enjoyed spending the rest of her life here but it was time to sweep that broken dream under the carpet.

About the only crumb of comfort she could find in this whole rotten mess was that at least she was denying him the pleasure of humiliating her in public. What really sickened her was the cold-blooded way he'd used her. And according to Pamela she was just the latest in a long line of victims. How any woman could bring herself to marry a man like that was beyond belief. There was no doubt in her mind now that she'd had a lucky escape. Old habits died hard and she doubted if a man with his predatory instincts would pay much attention to marriage vows.

'Avalon?'

She whirled in shocked surprise and saw Kirsty standing in the middle of the room, a sad smile on her face.

Her mouth dropped open and her eyes darted to the door, then back to Kirsty. 'How . . . how did you get in? The door is locked.'

'Och . . . I wouldn't be trusting the locks in this old house,' Kirsty said quietly. 'Sometimes they work. Sometimes they don't.'

'Did . . . did Fraser send you?' she asked suspiciously.

Kirsty shook her head. 'No one sent me. But Pamela is down there acting like the cat who's got the cream. She's been up here talking to you, hasn't she?'

'Yes, she has,' Avalon replied bitterly. 'She's been telling me a few home truths and the way I've been tricked.'

The older woman looked pained. 'No one has tricked you, my dear.'

'No?' She looked at Kirsty angrily. 'How about that so-called Fire Magic? It's nothing but marsh gas. Are you going to deny that?'

Kirsty sighed. 'Of course it's marsh gas. But the magic is what causes it to catch fire.'

'Well, it wasn't your friends the fairies,' she retorted angrily. 'It was old Gavin's cigarette-end.'

'Aye...' agreed Kirsty quietly. 'But who caused Gavin to be there at that exact moment in time?'

Avalon stared at her in frustration. 'Look... if you've come here to persuade me into going down you're wasting your time.'

Kirsty sighed and said gently, 'That's something you'll have to decide for yourself. Otherwise it means nothing. As for Pamela... well, she's as tricky as the lock on that door. I wouldn't be putting too much trust in the things she says.'

Angrily Avalon turned her back on her and stared out of the window in silence. She didn't want to talk about it any more. She just wanted this day and night to end. No one—not even Kirsty—was going to change her mind. That had always been her trouble. Listening to people with plausible tongues. People like her ex-boyfriend... Mr Smith in Portugal... Kirsty... Pamela...

Her train of thought hit the buffers. Pamela...?

She turned, but Kirsty had gone as silently as she'd appeared. Dammit! She wished she hadn't been so rude. Now, what was it she'd said about Pamela? Something about being as tricky as the lock on the door. Kirsty had tried to warn her about Pamela...not to trust her.

Yet Pamela had been so convincing, offering sympathy and help. Oh, yes, Mr Smith had offered sympathy and help. Let's not forget that.

She sat on the edge of the bed and chewed distractedly at her thumbnail. Supposing everything

Pamela had told her had been a pack of lies? Very well...what was her motive? To make sure that Avalon kept away from the Ceilidh. But if Fraser had promised to marry her, as she'd said, she had nothing to worry about. That could mean that Fraser had given no such promise. But time was running out for Fraser and he had to choose his wife tonight, while the Clan was gathered, as tradition demanded. Pamela just wanted to make sure that she had the field to herself.

The sudden insight into Pamela's duplicity forced her to her feet. The long-suffering fiancée prepared to forgive her man's transgressions while sympathising with his victims. That bitch had played the part brilliantly. And all the time it had been a cold and calculating attempt to undermine her rival's self-confidence. Of course the fact that her self-confidence had been teetering on the edge, thus making Pamela's job so much easier, didn't make it any less evil.

There was always the possibility that she was simply grasping at straws and that Pamela really was telling the truth, but the only way to find out was by going down there right now and confronting Fraser. She might end up in abject misery but that was a risk she'd have to take. This time she wasn't going to run away and hide. This time she was going to stay and fight.

Hurriedly she changed back into the dress, arranged the sash and brooch, had one final check in the mirror, then went to the door.

It was still locked! So how had Kirsty...?

She blinked at it in confusion for a moment, then turned the key and pulled the door open. She'd worry about it later. Right now she had other things on her mind.

For the moment the music had stopped but she could still hear the sound of loud conversation and laughter from the ballroom as she made her way downstairs. By the time she reached the hallway her stomach was fluttering with nerves and her mouth was dry. Resisting the urge to retreat upstairs in a funk she took a deep breath then, holding her head high, she walked across the hallway and through the wide doors into the ballroom.

Her sudden entrance caused a ripple of sound among the guests and from the corner of her eye she saw people turning to stare at her. At the far end, gathered in front of the huge fireplace, a group of distinguished-looking men and women guests were engaged in animated conversation with Fraser but they, too, turned to stare as she made her way towards them.

The journey seemed to take forever, every agonising step requiring all her reserves of courage and determination. Her heart pounded even faster as she neared Fraser. Oh God, how handsome he looked, resplendent in kilt and light blue tunic. But that look on his dark features? Was it pleasure, anger or, even worse, indifference? There was no clue to his feelings in that set expression, the tight line of his mouth or the reflected light in his blue eyes.

Pamela was clinging to his arm possessively and there was no doubt about her expression. Seething rage.

She stared back into those furious eyes calmly and said, 'Hello, Pamela. My headache has gone so I've

decided to come down and join in the fun after all.'
She smiled brightly at the assembled company, then
challenged Fraser softly, 'Well? Would you like to introduce me to your friends?'

Beneath her cool, collected exterior her insides were
shaking. Any second now her fragile imposture would
crack under the strain.

Fraser's eyes bored into hers, searching, seeking to
penetrate beyond the mask, then she saw the slight,
almost imperceptible tilt to his mouth. Murmuring an
apology to Pamela, he disengaged her arm from his,
then said loudly, 'I'm glad you finally made it,
caileagh bhan. We all thought you'd decided to go
for another swim.'

There was a ripple of laughter around the room and
she caught sight of Kirsty in the background, giving
her a smile of encouragement. Then someone pressed
a glass of whisky into her hand. Taking a tiny sip, she
savoured it for a moment, then nodded wisely. 'Very
nice. A single malt. Glenmorangie, I think.'

The men in the company looked at her in surprise
and a voice said, 'The lassie might be English but she
has an educated palate. She knows her whiskies.'

She took another sip, then replied lightly, 'I wish I
did. Actually, I saw the labels on the bottles when I
was in here this afternoon.'

Her admission drew a roar of laughter. 'At least
she's honest.'

Fraser smiled at her. He'd smiled at her before but
never like this. And his eyes were the warm blue of
a summer sky. The pounding of her heart grew
stronger, but not with fear and trepidation. This time
it was excitement.

Taking the glass from her hand he passed it to someone else then, with his arm firmly around her shoulder, he began the introductions.

'Cameron, may I introduce Miss Avalon Rivers?'

She found herself looking up at a tall, patrician man with grey hair. They shook hands then she smiled. '*Co as a tha sibh?*'

The man's eyes widened in surprise. '*A bheil Gaidhlig agaibh?*'

She struggled to find the right words. '*B...Beagan...Tha mi ag...*'

'You're learning?' he translated. His face cracked open in a smile and he turned to the others. 'She's learning the Gaelic! By the sound of her she'll be speaking it like a native soon.'

The rest of the introductions went rapidly. Too fast and too many names to remember. When they were finished Fraser led her by the hand to the centre of the floor, then held up a hand for silence. As soon as the noise had died away he withdrew a leather pouch from the pocket of his tunic and whispered to her, 'I'm proud of you, Avalon. Now, hold your head high. You're the most beautiful woman in this room and I want everyone to see what I'm about to do.'

Her body trembled like a delicate leaf in a breeze as he produced the glittering diamond and emerald necklace and gently placed it round her neck. He stepped back to admire the effect then, placing his hands lightly on her shoulders, he bent down and gave her a kiss of warm, sweet and loving tenderness.

Straightening up he stood for a moment like some proud, Celtic warrior surveying his followers then, in a voice which rang out with authority, he declared,

'This woman I choose as my wife.' He paused to ensure there was attentive silence, then he completed the traditional formality. 'If there be any among you here who dare to challenge her fitness to be the First Lady of this Clan, then speak now.'

The room remained hushed as he slowly turned, looking and listening for any sign of dissent, then he grinned and nodded. 'So be it. I take it that you all agree with my choice?'

The deafening roar of approval rattled the very chandeliers and he swept her protectively into his arms as the crowd surged around to congratulate them.

The uproar slowly died away, toasts were drunk and the band were limbering up for a night of festivities that would be talked about for generations to come.

Suddenly Kirsty was by their side, glass of whisky in one hand and inevitable roll-up stuck in the corner of her mouth. She was still wearing the same chunky old sweater and tweed skirt and Avalon simply couldn't imagine her in anything else. There was nothing refined or graceful about Kirsty but she was as comforting as a child's teddy bear or a hot water bottle in a cold bed.

The warm brown eyes smiled at her. 'Welcome to the Clan, *caileagh bhan*.'

She smiled back. 'Thanks, Kirsty. And thanks for coming to...'

Kirsty cut her off quickly and turned to Fraser. 'That was a fine speech you gave, Fraser. Under Clan law you and Avalon are now married but it might be a good idea to have the wedding sanctioned under civil law while we're here.' She looked at him keenly and lowered her voice. 'I'm thinking about that uncle of yours.'

Fraser nodded. 'Aye, Kirsty. As usual you're two steps ahead of everyone else.'

'Good,' Kirsty said cheerfully, beaming at both of them. 'Cameron is a Justice of the Peace. He'll be glad to perform the ceremony. I'll go and have a word in his ear now.'

Avalon was still trying to take it all in. She'd just become Fraser's wife. Another one of those mysterious Clan laws and customs. But, just in case there were any doubts as to the strict legality of such an arrangement, they were about to undergo another ceremony. She felt dizzy. She felt exhilarated. She needed to sit down and recover from the shock but there was little chance of that.

Some of her feelings transmitted themselves to Fraser and he squeezed her hand and looked down at her with concern. 'Do you feel all right? You've gone pale. We can put this off till later if you want.'

She took a deep breath and smiled. 'Don't worry about me, darling. It's just that it's all happening so fast. I'm still trying to get used to the idea of having you as my husband.' She took another deep breath and felt the colour come back to her cheeks.

There was another bout of handshakes and congratulations but it took Kirsty less than ten minutes to get the ceremony organised. Avalon chose an awe-struck but obviously delighted Aileen to be her bridesmaid while Big Duncan was roped in as Fraser's best man. Cameron, the Justice of the Peace, stood before them ready to begin when Fraser exclaimed, 'Damn! I haven't got a ring to give to Avalon.'

Kirsty stepped forward and held out her hand. 'Then it's lucky I brought this with me.' Her eyes, full of secrets, twinkled at Avalon. 'Don't worry. It'll be a perfect fit.'

Yes, of course it would be, Avalon told herself dreamily. If Kirsty said it, it must be so.

CHAPTER TEN

THE beach was bathed in soft moonlight and the sea stirred gently in its sleep. The wild, uninhibited music of the Ceilidh came faintly from the house beyond the trees and Fraser held her closely and murmured, 'If you're cold we'll go back in.'

Her hand reached up and her fingertips caressed his lips. 'Not yet, darling. I want to get used to the idea of having you all to myself at last. Anyway... you've got a lot of explaining to do.'

His mouth came down and teased hers, then he muttered hoarsely, 'I can think of better ways to occupy our time.' His hands tightened around her, impatient, driven by the force of his need, and her own pulse quickened in response, then he released her reluctantly and laughed huskily. 'My God, Avalon! Those wonderful green eyes... that delectable little body... The very sound of your voice does things to me. I think you really are a sea-witch sent to drive me mad with desire.'

They resumed their walk along the beach, his arm around her shoulder, her arm around his waist. The lights of the village reflected in long golden streaks across the water of the bay. Just to make sure this wasn't all a fantastic dream her fingers went to her throat and felt the necklace. 'It's so wonderful here,' she sighed.

'You're quite willing to spend the rest of your life here?' he asked quietly.

'Oh, yes, darling,' she breathed. 'It's strange...but I...I feel as if I belonged here...as if I'd always been a part of this place. I love it... almost as much as I love you.'

'Aye...' He sounded pleased. 'That's what I had to be sure of. Most people come here for a holiday. They stay two weeks and think it's wonderful. Then they start to miss the bustle and excitement of the city. I was afraid that might happen to you. I couldn't have stood it if you'd been miserable for the things you missed.'

She snorted. 'Those people are fools. I've had more excitement here than I ever had at home. The people are friendlier and who needs all the hassle of traffic jams and air you can't breathe without coughing and bored check-out girls and muggings and...?' She stopped and smiled up at him. 'Believe me. This is paradise and I never want to leave.'

His arm tightened around her affectionately. 'That's how I hoped you'd feel. But right until the very end I still wasn't sure. But then you proved your commitment when I discovered that you'd been learning Gaelic. That made a big impression on everybody back there. I've never seen old Cameron look so pleased about anything in his life.'

She passed it over lightly. 'It's no big deal. If I'd wanted to live in France I'd have learnt to speak French.'

'Aye. But you wanted to live here so you learnt our language. That was all the proof I needed.' He looked down at her, his puzzled frown clear in the moonlight. 'Who's been teaching you? Mrs MacKay?'

'No. It was young Jamie. That's why I've been seeing him most evenings. But I told him it was to be a secret between the pair of us. I . . . I suppose I was afraid of making a fool of myself.'

He laughed easily. 'No one would have laughed at you, my delicious little mermaid. I'd have taught you myself if you'd have only asked.'

'I . . . I wanted it to be a surprise.'

He gave her a friendly growl. 'Aye. You're full of surprises, aren't you? When I first saw you lying in Kirsty's cottage——'

'I was naked,' she interrupted, then she smiled at the recollection. 'There was no one more surprised than I was. I saw you and I thought I was dreaming.'

They strolled for a few more minutes in contented silence, listening to the gentle lap of the water on the beach, then she stopped and looked up at him in mock-accusation. 'You weren't very nice to me the next morning, were you? I thought you were a bad-tempered ogre.'

'And you were a bad-tempered little city girl with a chip on her shoulder,' he teased. 'You nearly bit my head off and told me to keep my hands to myself.'

She poked a finger playfully in his ribs. 'I had good reason to be annoyed. It isn't every day a girl wakes up to be told that she's been brought by the fairies to marry a man she's never laid eyes on before. And when that man starts pawing you...well, how did you expect me to act?' She teased him with a smile. 'Things are different now, though. You can paw me any time you like.'

'Aye...' he agreed with genuine contrition. 'I treated you roughly. But in spite of that we still managed to fall in love with each other, didn't we?'

'Hmm...' She considered his statement with a thoughtful little smile on her face, then declared,

'Well, I know when I fell in love but I don't know about you.'

He stroked her long, blonde hair and felt the silky texture between his fingers and thumb, then playfully kissed the tip of her nose. 'It was the very first night. In the library. In front of a large fire. Your skin was golden and you were like a ripe and juicy little peach just ready for eating.'

The memory sent a little shiver down her spine and she murmured, 'Yes... I seem to remember that night. Only vaguely, mind you,' she added with a furrow on her brow.

'Then I'll take great pleasure in jolting your memory when we get back to the house,' he vowed in her ear. 'We'll go over it step by step. All night if necessary.'

'Yes...' she said thoughtfully. 'I suppose that might help.'

He drew her closer and kissed her gently on the eyelids and the mouth, then said huskily, 'The Ceilidh won't finish till after midnight. I think we should pay a visit to the library right now.'

She laughed. 'We'd better not. I'm sure I saw Aileen sneaking in there with her boyfriend earlier on.'

'Damn...' he growled. 'That's the trouble with teenagers nowadays. No respect.' He chuckled softly. 'Aye... we'd better not spoil their fun.'

'Good,' she said calmly. 'That means you've plenty of time to tell me about Pamela. She disappeared right after you gave me this necklace.'

'Aye...' he growled. 'I dare say she'll be halfway to Edinburgh by now with her tail between her legs.'

His tone surprised her, especially after the tales Pamela had spun. 'You really don't like her, do you?'

He shrugged. 'Let's just say I feel sorry for her.'

'Well, I don't,' she declared heatedly. 'And neither would you if you'd heard the things she said. The lies she told.'

He laughed cynically. 'Aye . . . I guessed she'd been up to see you.'

'You guessed?'

'When I came to fetch you down you'd locked yourself in,' he reminded her grimly. 'You told me to go away. That's when I knew that she'd got at you.'

'Oh, she got at me all right,' she said bitterly. 'She's such a great actress she had me feeling sorry for her. Why didn't you warn me about her? When I asked about her you said it was none of my business.'

He soothed her annoyance away with a kiss, then said, 'I asked you to trust me, remember?'

'Yes, darling. I did trust you. Even though I can't understand the complicated machinations of your mind. I can only hope you had a very good reason.'

His blue eyes looked honestly and directly into hers. 'She was your final test, Avalon. Pamela is a manipulative schemer. If you couldn't handle someone like her it would have been unfair of me to ask you to marry me. I'd have been pitching you into a lifestyle you hated and I love you too much for that. The First Lady of any Clan has to be able to see through pretension, affectation and deceit and come out on top. Because of your position you'll be under pressure from people like her a lot of the time. Life with me might not be quite the bed of roses you imagined.'

'I'm not looking for a bed of roses, darling,' she said with quiet sincerity. 'Your love is all I'll ever need.'

He wrapped his arms around her and nuzzled her ear with his lips. 'It's yours forever.'

She felt a sudden twinge of conscience but decided to ignore it for the moment. 'Did Pamela ever mean anything to you? She told me that you'd promised to marry her. Was she making it all up?'

'Not exactly,' he admitted quietly.

'Oh...?' She regarded him suspiciously. 'What does "not exactly" mean? Did you or did you not promise to marry her?'

'Yes. I did.'

'I see...' Some of the enchantment seemed to go out of the evening.

'She was twelve years old at the time,' he added ruefully. He saw her look of amazement and he explained, 'I was studying for my degree at Edinburgh University at the time. I became quite friendly with a fellow student called Harry Russell. His parents had a large estate just outside Edinburgh. I was in student digs but Harry's parents insisted that I spend my weekends at their place.'

He paused reflectively, then went on. 'They were a nice couple and I still keep in touch with them and Harry. I returned their hospitality by inviting them all up here during the holidays. It was a friendly, cosy arrangement except for one thing. Pamela. She was Harry's young sister.' He stopped and gave her a perplexed frown. 'Tell me, Avalon, is it normal for a twelve-year-old girl to get a crush on a man of twenty-one?'

'Well, when I was twelve I was madly in love with an American pop idol,' she admitted uncomfortably.

'That's different,' he pointed out. 'He was probably just a poster on your bedroom wall. I was living under the same roof as the damn girl. Have you any idea how embarrassing it is having a twelve-year-old girl flirting and fluttering her eyelashes at you? Never when her parents were around, though. She was too clever for that.' He sighed with exasperation at the memory, then went on, 'I put up with it because I thought it was all a childish game with her and when she coyly made me promise to wait until she was old enough to marry me I agreed.'

Avalon already had a mental image of a spoilt, scheming little brat in need of a sound spanking.

Fraser laughed, mocking his own stupidity. 'Perhaps I should have put her straight there and then, but I was scared she'd burst into tears if I did. Anyway, you expect kids to outgrow their childish fantasies, don't you? Not her, though. After I got my degree I went to work abroad. When I came home years later I renewed my friendship with her parents and told them they were welcome to visit here any time they liked.'

'And Pamela would be all grown up by then?' she asked, remembering just how attractive Pamela was.

He nodded. 'I didn't recognise her until she opened her mouth and began gushing all over me.' He seemed to shudder at the memory. 'She might have grown up but it was soon apparent that she was nothing but gloss and varnish hiding an ugly soul full of ruthless ambition. I let her know, in as polite a way as possible, that I wasn't interested in her, but she's one of those people who can't take no for an answer. She's been spoilt all her life and it's inconceivable to her that she could be denied anything she'd set her sights on.'

'I suppose she took your invitation to visit a bit too literally?' she asked, getting the picture now.

'Aye, she did,' growled Fraser. 'She's been coming up here regularly. Usually for a weekend at a time.

She's got an inborn talent for annoying everyone and making a perfect nuisance of herself by throwing her weight about.'

'And you've been too much of a gentleman to tell her that she's not welcome any more?' she suggested sympathetically.

He smiled in bitter recollection. 'It isn't easy. I like her parents. I was more concerned about saving their feelings than I was about hurting hers. I don't think they know what a real little horror they've raised.'

Well, 'Lady' Pamela had certainly got the message this evening, Avalon told herself. In spite of her lying and scheming, Fraser was one prize she'd failed to get. No doubt she was already sharpening her claws and looking for some more susceptible victim.

She started to say something else but he placed the palm of his hand over her mouth and jokingly threatened her. 'No more about Pamela. Mention her name again this evening and I'll have my wicked way with you. That'll give you something else to think about.'

He took his hand away and she looked at him meekly. 'I was just going to say that if she ever showed her face here again I'd scratch her eyes out.' She lowered her eyes and smiled. 'As for having your wicked way with me, I'm just a poor defenceless girl and you're so strong and powerful and...'

'Don't tempt fate,' he said huskily. 'There's a very inviting grassy bank over there.'

She pulled his head down and planted a quick kiss on his mouth. 'Let's wait till we get back, darling. Clan Chiefs shouldn't go rolling about on the grass in their best kilts. It isn't dignified.'

The moonlight glistened on his dark hair and reflected the amusement in his blue eyes. 'This particular Clan Chief places dignity a poor second to passion. Especially with someone as bewitchingly beautiful as you in his arms.'

She looked at him closely, then murmured, 'I wonder what colour our children's eyes will be. Yours are blue and mine are green.'

'All the girls will have green eyes and all the boys blue,' he asserted firmly.

'All?' She laughed. 'How many were you thinking of having?'

'Well . . . it's a big house with plenty of rooms.'

'Yes. Twenty at least.'

He stroked her cheek gently and she could almost feel the waves of loving warmth surge through her body. That simple touch told her more about his feelings for her than any amount of words.

'Two will do fine,' he whispered. 'A girl as lovely as her mother and a boy to grow up strong and fearless—the future Chief of the Clan.'

'I'll give you them, darling. I promise,' she whispered back. 'I'll give you children to be proud of.' She was silent for a moment, then she said determinedly, 'I want Kirsty to be their godmother. Will you ask her for me?'

Her choice met with his instant approval. 'Of course I will. It'll please her a lot.'

Yes, she thought, she owed everything to Kirsty. If it hadn't been for her she wouldn't be standing here now, making plans for the future with the man she loved. If Kirsty hadn't come to the room and warned her about trusting Pamela . . . Once again she pushed the guilty thought aside.

They began strolling again, their arms around each other. This was a moment, an evening in her life to be cherished—to remember in years to come when the snow was thick and the logs were burning bright in the fireplace. Nothing should be allowed to spoil it. And yet she had to know...

'It's all making sense to me now, darling,' she said enigmatically.

He looked down at her fondly. 'What makes sense?'

'The things Kirsty was talking about when I first woke up in her cottage.' She furrowed her brow in concentration. 'She said that I'd arrived just in time. The Clan was safe from disaster now. It...it has something to do with your uncle, hasn't it?'

Fraser grunted. 'I suppose Pamela told you about it?'

She smiled up at him innocently. 'You mentioned her name. Not me.'

'Aye...well, there's no secret. There's nothing to hide,' he said easily. 'I had to be married by my thirty-fifth birthday. If I'm not in a position to produce an heir by then the Chieftainship goes to the next in line of succession, who happens to be my uncle.' He made a sound of contempt. 'That's the disaster Kirsty was talking about. If he got his hands on this place half the people in the village would be put out on the street and their houses sold as holiday homes to his clients down south.'

'I see...' she murmured. 'And you couldn't possibly let that happen, could you?'

'No, Avalon,' he agreed gravely. 'I couldn't.'

So Pamela had been right, she thought. He had to get married. She bit her lip, then screwed up her courage. 'Does that mean you would have married Pamela? Only out of necessity?' she added awkwardly. 'I mean, just to keep your position as Chief?'

She heard his sharp intake of breath and she immediately regretted her insensitivity at putting him in such a spot. 'Look...' she said hastily. 'It doesn't really matter.'

'It does matter.' He looked down at her in tortured silence for a moment, then confessed quietly, 'Yes. I'd have married her. Much as I detest her, I'd have gone through with it. There are times when duty demands sacrifices.'

And it was a sacrifice she'd almost forced him to make through her own blindness, she thought bitterly. 'Pamela must have known that,' she murmured. 'It would explain why she was so desperate to keep me away from the Ceilidh.'

He nodded in agreement. 'Aye. That's the way her mind works.' Suddenly the wicked grin was back on his face. 'Now, I warned you once. I told you what would happen if you mentioned her name again.'

'I know... I know...' She tried to wriggle out of his grasp but he bent down and kissed her with a passion fierce enough to drive every thought from her mind. His hungry mouth left her lips bruised and aching and she arced her head back with a delicious shudder as he covered her slim neck and bare shoulders with tremor-inducing kisses.

At last he straightened up and as she recovered her breath he said hoarsely, 'You're gorgeous enough by daylight. In the moonlight you're spell-binding.'

She felt a hard lump in her throat. 'I... I think we'd better change the subject before we start forgetting where we are.' She held her hand out. 'Can you tell me how Kirsty just happened to have this ring with her? Look at it! It's beautiful. And it's a perfect size! Just as she said.'

He grinned, his white teeth flashing in the moon-light. 'Who knows? Kirsty can't be explained. If she started walking on water no one around here would be the least bit surprised.'

The feeling of guilt overcame her again and she said quietly, 'I'm going to mention Pamela again.'

He groaned. 'If you really must.'

'Yes, darling, I must. I'm going to start this marriage as I mean to continue. There'll never be any secrets between us from now on. I've got a confession to make.'

He clapped a hand to his brow in horror. 'You're already married, with two kids?'

'I'm serious.' She drew a deep breath. 'You said that dealing with Pamela was my final test. Well . . . I didn't deal with her. She had me completely fooled. If it hadn't been for Kirsty coming up and telling me not to trust her I'd still be sitting in my room. I wouldn't be wearing this necklace nor this wedding ring.'

'Kirsty went to your room?' He looked and sounded puzzled.

'Yes.'

'When, exactly?'

'About five minutes after you came up and banged on my door.'

He shook his head. 'You must have imagined it. Kirsty never left the ballroom while I was there. Cameron will testify to that. The three of us were discussing scholarship grants for some of the village children when they go to university.'

She smiled. 'I'm sorry, darling. You're wrong. She came to my room. Granted, it was only for a few minutes but we . . . we . . .' Her voice trailed off. She remembered the locked door. And she hadn't heard Kirsty enter...nor leave. She swallowed nervously. 'You...you may be right. I...I could have imagined it after all.'

Ahead of them, across the bay beyond the village and high up on the Nevay, a tall blue flame flickered briefly then died. Fraser reached for her and she snuggled into his chest. 'That must have been Kirsty's fairies celebrating,' he murmured softly in her ear.

'Yes...' She sighed with pleasure. 'I expect it was.'

Legends and fairies, she thought. A woman who could foretell the future and who could be in two places at once. She seemed to hear the laughter of tiny voices carried in the still night air. There really was something magical about this place, she told herself dreamily. But this was the real magic...being in the arms of the man you loved.

'Let's go home now, darling,' she murmured up at him. 'It's getting cold.'

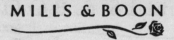

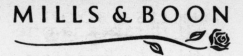

MILLS & BOON

Next Month's Romances

Each month you can choose from a wide variety of romance with Mills & Boon. Below are the new titles to look out for next month.

THE SHINING OF LOVE	Emma Darcy
A BRIEF ENCOUNTER	Catherine George
SECRET OBSESSION	Charlotte Lamb
A VERY SECRET AFFAIR	Miranda Lee
DEAREST LOVE	Betty Neels
THE WEDDING EFFECT	Sophie Weston
UNWELCOME INVADER	Angela Devine
UNTOUCHED	Sandra Field
THIEF OF HEARTS	Natalie Fox
FIRE AND SPICE	Karen van der Zee
JUNGLE FEVER	Jennifer Taylor
BEYOND ALL REASON	Cathy Williams
FOREVER ISN'T LONG ENOUGH	Val Daniels
TRIUMPH OF LOVE	Barbara McMahon
IRRESISTIBLE ATTRACTION	Alison Kelly
FREE TO LOVE	Alison York

Available from WH Smith, John Menzies, Volume One, Forbuoys, Martins, Woolworths, Tesco, Asda, Safeway and other paperback stockists.

"All it takes is one letter to trigger a romance"

Sealed with a Kiss—don't miss this exciting new mini-series every month.

All the stories involve a relationship which develops as a result of a letter being written—we know you'll love these new heart-warming romances.

And to make them easier to identify, all the covers in this series are a passionate pink!

Available now   **Price: £1.90**

MILLS & BOON

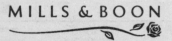

To celebrate 10 years of Temptation we are giving away a host of tempting prizes...

10 prizes of FREE Temptation Books for a whole year

— **plus** —

10 runner up prizes of *Thorntons* delicious Temptations Chocolates

Enter our Temptation Wordsearch Quiz Today and Win!

10th All you have to do is complete the wordsearch puzzle below and send it to us by 31 May 1995.

The first 10 correct entries drawn from the bag will each win 12 month's free supply of exciting Temptation books (4 books every month with a total annual value of around £100).

The second 10 correct entries drawn will each win a 200g box of *Thorntons* Temptations chocolates.

I	F	G	N	I	T	I	C	X	E
A	O	X	O	C	A	I	N	S	S
N	O	I	T	A	T	P	M	E	T
N	B	V	E	N	R	Y	N	X	E
I	R	O	A	M	A	S	N	Y	R
V	C	M	T	I	U	N	N	F	U
E	O	H	U	O	T	M	V	E	T
R	N	X	U	R	E	Y	S	I	N
S	L	S	M	A	N	F	L	Y	E
A	T	O	N	U	T	R	X	L	V
R	U	O	M	U	H	I	A	A	D
Y	W	D	Y	O	F	I	M	K	A

TEMPTATION   ROMANTIC
SEXY   SENSUOUS
FUN   ADVENTURE
EXCITING   HUMOUR
TENTH   ANNIVERSARY

PLEASE TURN OVER FOR ENTRY DETAILS

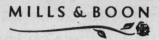

MILLS & BOON

HOW TO ENTER

10ª All the words listed overleaf below the wordsearch puzzle, are hidden in the grid. You can find them by reading the letters forward, backwards, up and down, or diagonally. When you find a word, circle it or put a line through it.

Don't forget to fill in your name and address in the space below then put this page in an envelope and post it today (you don't need a stamp). Closing date 31st May 1995.

Temptation Wordsearch,
FREEPOST,
P.O. Box 344,
Croydon,
Surrey
CR9 9EL

COMP395

Are you a Reader Service Subscriber?   Yes ☐   No ☐

Ms/Mrs/Miss/Mr _____

Address _____

_____

_____ Postcode _____

mps
MAILING
PREFERENCE
SERVICE